Celestial Journeys, Book 4

Digital Dreams

Marlow Miller

Table of Contents

CELESTIAL VERSE FUN FACTS 4

CHAPTER 1: AN UNPLEASANT LANDING 13

CHAPTER 2: A REALLY BAD FIRST DAY 19

CHAPTER 3: NOTICING TALENT..25

CHAPTER 4: A FANTASTIC OFFER 31

CHAPTER 5: HACKING HEAVEN..37

CHAPTER 6: DON'T GET CAUGHT 43

CHAPTER 7: ODD ORDERS 49

CHAPTER 8: ACTUALLY A BAD GUY..55

CHAPTER 9: TROUBLING TROUBLE 61

CHAPTER 10: A SURPRISING IDENTITY 67

CHAPTER 11: A SECRET PLOT 73

CHAPTER 12: THE LONELY LEADER 79

CHAPTER 13: A GADGET REVOLUTION 85

CHAPTER 14: SUDDENLY SAVED 91

CHAPTER 15: A GOOD COMPROMISE 97

EPILOGUE..103

To my mom, Gloria, for the inspiration to write books.

To my grandchildren, who continue to inspire me to write stories for your imagination.

To my readers, hope you find your loyal byt bug soon!

CELESTIAL VERSE

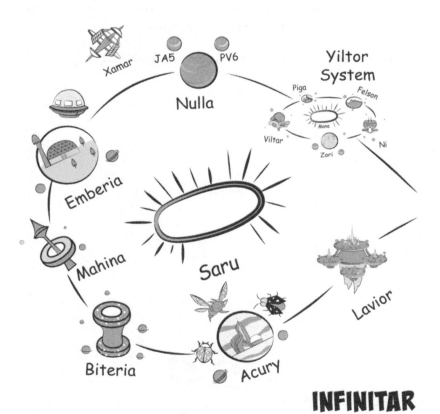

Xamar · JA5 · PV6 · **Nulla**

Yiltor System — Piga · Felson · Mana · Viltar · Zori · Ni

Emberia

Saru

Mahina

Biteria

Acury

Lavior

INFINITAR

Infinitar Galaxy : 5 years per loops, 10 years rotation

Yiltor System : 1 year rotation

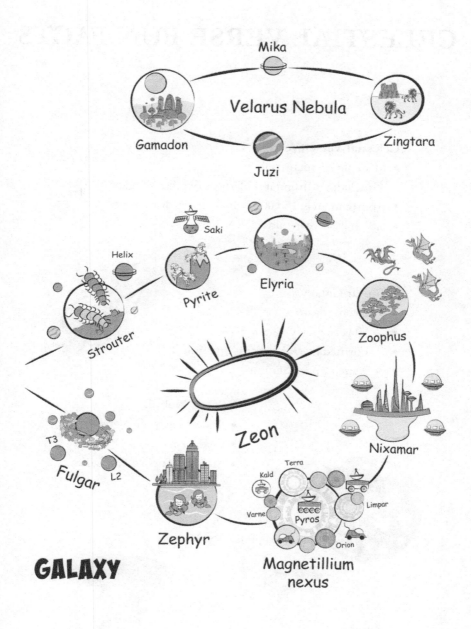

Mika

Velarus Nebula

Gamadon

Zingtara

Juzi

Saki

Helix

Pyrite

Elyria

Strouter

Zoophus

Zeon

Nixamar

T3

Fulgar

L2

Zephyr

Terra

Kald

Varne

Pyros

Limpar

Orion

Magnetillium
nexus

GALAXY

CELESTIAL VERSE FUN FACTS

Celestial Verse (Verse)
- Made up of many star systems
  o including: Infinitar, Velarus, Loximar, Bendax
- Approximately 150,000 light-years in diameter
- 6.81 billion years old

Infinitar Galaxy
- 2 center stars
- 10 year galaxy rotation
- Formed by star systems collision
- Xamar Space Station

Velarus Nebula
- Oldest galaxy in Verse
- 3-year rotation
- Stellar Camp on Gamadon

Acury
- Cyber planet
- Migrated Byt bugs

Bitoria
- Spiral layers
- Hatches Byt bugs

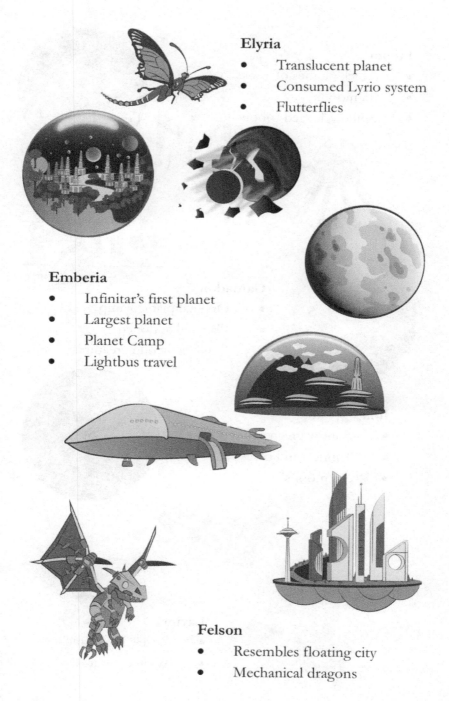

Elyria
- Translucent planet
- Consumed Lyrio system
- Flutterflies

Emberia
- Infinitar's first planet
- Largest planet
- Planet Camp
- Lightbus travel

Felson
- Resembles floating city
- Mechanical dragons

Fulgar

- Thick plumes of rocks
- 45 moons
- Spindly, legged robots

Gamadon

- Original planet camp
- Planet abandoned
- Rumors of odd creatures

Juzi

- Bumpy green surface
- Tunnels and caves
- No moons

Lavior

- Levels like branches
- Wing creatures

Mahina

- Small planet top
- Satellite bottom
- Wonky, wobbly spin

Magnetillium System

- Strong magnetic field
- Planets cluster
- Pink surfaces
- Space vehicles
- Pink serpent, Skarion

Mika

- 50% ice; huge ice caves
- Snow creatures-Dragor
- Snow tribes in ice caves

Ni

- Egg-shaped clusters
- Stuck during collision
- Quiet, very little wind

Nixamar
- Manufacture space vehicles
- Maintain Lightbuses
- From Loximar galaxy

Nulla
- Mountains and moons inside
- Translucent
- Swirling light shows

Piga
- Yiltor's Smallest planet
- 50-100 feet spire cities

Pyrite
- Broken planet stuck to side
- Caves and Mountains
- Dragons, Large horse creatures

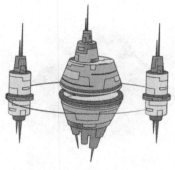

Saki

- Pyrite's satellite moon
- Infinitar's collision pulled into Pyrite's atmosphere

Strouter

- Desert planet
- Supersonic winds up to 1,100 miles per hour
- Large Sandipedes
- Violent wind and sandstorms
- Helix – Strouter's only moon

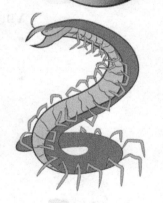

Terra

- Largest Magnetillium planet
- Strong magnetic force
- Planets stuck to its sides
- Pink serpent, Skarion

Viltar

- Ornate planet structure
- Great tunneling caves
- Many moons, up to 100

Yiltor System

- Pulled in to Infinitar's rotation during collision
- Travels Infinitar's double-loop rotation
- 1 small center star
- 1 year rotation

Zephyr

- Water planet
- 95% surface oceans
- Mermaid creatures
- Floating cities

Zingtora

- Futuristic plants
- Abandoned Zoo farms
- Monkey and lion creatures spotted

Zoophus

- Plant planet
- Avatar like plants
- Mini dragons
- Very mountainous

Zori

- Yiltor's largest planet
- Atmosphere like Emberia
- Sky-creatures seen in clouds

Chapter 1:

An Unpleasant Landing

"We're here!" Levi Helix laughs as the ship starts to lower toward the planet. From the moment he was chosen for Acury, Levi has barely been able to sleep because of all of the excitement. He went to Planet Camp hoping that he'd get to go to the digital world, and this is a dream come true.

The other kids chosen for Acury storm to the nearest window with him, watching as they drift down through pixelated clouds. Below them is a vast digital city, so much bigger than the one they saw at Planet Camp.

"Wow," Levi breathes, holding his hand against the window's glass. "That is the coolest thing I have ever seen."

"Children, please line up," says a voice over the ship's announcement system. "Ensure that you have your baggage ready to be checked. No liquids, no additional accessories, and no sharp objects on your person."

"Huh?" A few kids, including Levi, frown up at the speaker, wondering what all those rules are about.

Still, everyone prepares their stuff and gets ready to disembark, standing in the landing room to wait for the ship to get down to the surface. Levi has put his hood down over his shoulders, his dark fringe still hanging over one of his eyes.

He wonders how long they'll have to wait before the ship lands on the surface of the planet. He really wants to get started with his training. Perhaps they'll learn how to hack computers or to build huge digital buildings. Maybe they'll be taught how to make new software... and their own games... and their own holo-characters! He's been thinking about all of these things on the planet-ship, and he doesn't know how he'd ever choose between them.

Hopefully, he doesn't have to.

"Please prepare to disembark," the voice over the speaker system says, immediately making everyone confused. They're still at least 2,000 feet above the surface of the planet. They can't exactly just step outside, fall all that way, and hope to land safely.

The kids start to whisper among each other, all insisting they're not going to be parachuting to the ground.

But the landing room's door opens, a rush of air flying into the ship. Levi's hair is instantly whipped back from his dark eyes, and he holds up his hand to try and block some of the wind.

Outside, there are several hovering platforms, similar to the ones that were at Planet Camp.

"Oh," Levi laughs, running forward to jump onto one of them, but a huge siren starts screaming through the room. Flashing red lights fill the whole place, coming from the platform.

A new voice comes through the announcement system, robotic and strict.

"Do not leave your place in the line. Remain in line. Proceed to platforms in an orderly fashion, one at a time. Get back in line immediately."

Levi doesn't like what's going on. It already looks like this place is going to have a lot more security and a lot more rules than he thought. That's no fun. Levi loves freedom. He can't imagine living in a place where he doesn't have any at all.

Still, Levi doesn't argue. He steps back in line, and immediately, the flashing lights and sirens disappear.

One by one, the kids get onto a platform, which takes them down to the surface of the planet. Levi gets onto his platform sixth. He's already bored, but he's trying to give all of this a chance. It could be that the people of Acury are just worried about security against outsiders. Surely it won't all be like this.

The platforms gently take the kids down to one of the digital streets. The city really does resemble the one at Planet Camp a lot. All of the streets have lights that run through them and make little networks of light everywhere the kids step on them. The buildings are huge and covered in LED lights that make all kinds of riveting colors.

Levi stares at everything around him, his heart lifting. This place is so awesome that it's not even that bad if there are a few rules. There's so much to see and explore all around him that it'll take a whole lifetime to see all of it.

Suddenly, a small mechanical bug zooms in from around the corner, stopping in front of the crowd of kids. It uses an infrared laser to scan all of them.

"Children, please form an orderly line and enter the building straight ahead of you," a robotic voice says, coming from the bug itself. "Do not veer off in any other direction. Do not attempt to leave the area. Follow the surveillance byt at all times."

There's another round of whispers among all the kids. Levi leans toward Luna, the girl standing closest to him.

"Is it just me, or is this a little crazy?" he asks her in a whisper as they all start lining up again. "Kind of seems like a prison, doesn't it?"

"Mm," Luna agrees, but she is distracted by all the lights. A little bit of surveillance doesn't bother her that much. It's safer if the adults know where they are and what they're doing. Especially if the adults themselves aren't around. Who knows what kind of trouble kids could get into on their own?

The new colonists march after the byt, some of them more eagerly than others. A few times, Levi considers simply walking away, into the city. After all, how is a bug going to stop him?

But he doesn't know what's out there yet, or how anything works. He doesn't know where he's going to live or if he needs any money or how training is going to go. Levi decides that he'll behave himself for now, but if things stay like this, he's definitely going to become a rebel.

Levi wants to be a great digital inventor. To do that, he needs the freedom to explore and to make new things. That's why he wanted to come to Acury. If he can't invent, then he'll have to find a way out of this situation.

They are ushered into a room with a big screen. There's barely enough space for everyone. It's dark until one huge light above them flashes on, making everyone cover their eyes for a few seconds.

The screen flickers and switches on. There's a lady's face on it, but she's clearly a digital image and not a real person. She has blue eyes that study the children closely and a strange, spaced-out smile. When she speaks, everyone is sure that she's definitely not a real person. She sounds exactly like a robot.

"Good day, New Colonists," she says, nodding to each of the kids in the room. "Welcome to Neo Aurora, Acury's greatest digital city."

Pictures of the city appear in the background: close-ups of huge digital buildings, screens, and neon signs. The kids start to whisper among themselves, but the lady on the screen immediately lifts her finger to her mouth to make them quiet.

"Please pay attention," she insists, sounding both friendly and angry at the same time. It's a very odd combination. "It is crucial that you follow *all* regulations of the Council of the City of Neo Aurora while you live here. These regulations are numerous and must be memorized within one week of arrival."

This time, everyone is too shocked to whisper among themselves. They're all staring at the screen like she's speaking in gibberish. The robot lady ignores the children and continues.

"Each of you will be assigned an apartment in the Starting Building," she explains, a picture of a tall, light-covered building in the middle of the city behind her. "There, you will receive your *Book of Rules, Regulations, and General Guidelines*, or the RRGG. This book is very important, and you must study it."

Levi is staring at her along with everyone else. This definitely isn't going as planned. This place has more rules than jail. It looks like there's no way he'll be able to become an inventor on Acury.

Chapter 2:

A Really Bad First Day

Levi's apartment is on the 54th floor of the Starting Building. It has so much security it's almost strange, and one of the byts has followed him all the way. At least the apartment itself is nice. It has a little kitchen with a food and drink dispenser, a bathroom, a big bedroom, and a lounge.

"Are you really going to follow me everywhere?" Levi grumbles at the byt, which is hovering just over his shoulder. "I can't switch you off? Ask you to leave?"

"Current schedule requires reading the Neo Aurora RRGG," the byt replies, completely ignoring Levi's questions. "The Neo Aurora RRGG can be found on your bedside table. You have one hour of reading scheduled."

"There's a schedule?" Levi moans, stretching the last word out as he stomps into the bedroom with his suitcase. "I mean, I guess, schedules are like... normal, but... Why do I have a reading schedule? What... What else is on the schedule?"

"This evening's schedule is well-planned and rigorous," the byt buzzes, creating a hologram in front of it. "One hour of reading the Neo Aurora RRGG, twenty minutes for unpacking, five-minute bathroom break, half an hour dinner, fifteen minutes of personal free time in the apartment lounge, fifteen minutes for an evening shower, and another half an hour reading time before bed, approved book of choice."

"What?" Levi almost yells as he stares at the hologram. He can't believe what he's seeing. *"Scheduled bathroom breaks?* That's got to be a joke, right? That's not real. How is this schedule even a little fair?"

"This evening's schedule is well-planned and—" the byt begins, repeating itself.

"No, I get it, you don't have to say the whole thing again," Levi interrupts, holding up his hand so that the byt will stop talking. "You're not very well built, are you?"

This time, the byt doesn't answer, although it does look for a second like its feelings have been hurt.

Levi shakes his head, deciding that he's not going to follow the schedule. Instead, he starts opening his suitcase to unpack his things. Immediately, a siren starts going off, coming from the surveillance byt, and it flashes red lights all around the room.

"Do not deviate," it says angrily, over and over. "Do not deviate."

"Okay, whoa, fine," Levi scoffs, walking over to his bedside table. There's a huge book on top of it. At least 500 pages. "I'll read!"

The byt quickly calms down and flies toward Levi to hover above his head. Levi sighs, picking up the book and flipping through, just to see what it looks like. There are so many different headings and chapters and rules. He has no idea how he'll learn all of it.

That night, Levi follows the schedule unhappily, doing exactly what the byt says he should. By the time he goes to bed, he's bristling with anger. He can't live like this. It's ridiculous.

In the morning, the byt blares an alarm again, this time with a green light dancing above its head. Groggily, Levi opens his eyes and peers at it.

"Do you have a snooze button?" he grumbles, reaching up to swat at the thing. The byt easily outmaneuvers his hand, still blaring the alarm.

"It is time to get up," it says, zooming around Levi's head insistently. "It is time to get up!"

"Okay, okay, fine!" Levi snaps, sitting up and throwing his legs out of the bed. "Look, I'm up, all right? I'm awake!"

"Today's schedule is well-planned and rigorous," the byt announces after it stops the alarm, shining a hologram from its head. Levi stares at the schedule miserably, knowing that he can't ignore it or the byt will make too much noise for him to handle.

Levi suffers through the morning routine. The surveillance byt follows him everywhere, except when he has a five-minute bathroom break. In there, Levi has some time to think. He really would prefer to escape this problem, but he doesn't know how.

"It is time for training, Levi Helix," the surveillance byt buzzes from outside the bathroom door. "Please follow."

Levi sighs and leaves the bathroom, trudging after the byt and grumbling under his breath. This whole thing is no fun at all.

The byt leads him out of the apartment and onto a floating platform that carries him through the streets at an impressive speed. That's at least one cool thing, even if it's scheduled just like everything else.

Levi wonders if he could reprogram the platform so that he could fly freely. If he ever gets the chance, he wants to try it out. It seems like it would be the most fun thing ever to just zoom across the city whenever and however he wants. But he'll figure that out eventually. For now, he has to do what the byt says or it will wail and cry again.

The platform lands outside of a square, boring building with the words "Training Building" in a white light above the front door.

"Please enter," the byt commands when the platform lands. "You are already 37.454 seconds behind schedule. Further delays cannot be allowed."

Levi rolls his eyes. "Can't you relax for a second? It's not that serious."

"Relaxation is not scheduled until this evening at 18:45," the byt answers, making Levi sigh. He walks inside of the training building, wondering if this will be any better. Inside, there's a long hall lined with computers. All of the other new kids are already sitting in their spots, their byts hovering over their shoulders.

Once Levi sits down, two people come walking into the hall. The first is a man with a bright smile, thick-rimmed glasses, and short blonde hair. His name is Sable Armitage, and he's in charge of training new colonists. He's wearing the standard Acury clothes: silver, metallic shirt and pants that seem to change colors as he moves. It's Levi's personal favorite thing about the planet so far.

Behind him is a girl called Juniper Lumin, probably a few years older than Levi, though she's wearing a hooded sweatshirt in that same metallic silver color. She has lilac-colored hair and big hazel eyes that make her look like she's easy to talk to and younger than she really is.

She has already spotted Levi, sitting in the back corner grumpily. He was over 30 seconds late, something that is entirely against regulation. But Juniper is sure that Sable will be patient and forgiving, given that it's the first training session. Her own byt is sitting on her shoulder comfortably, scratching at its camera lenses that look like eyes.

"Good morning, new ones!" Sable calls out as she grins with a laugh, looking pointedly at Levi. "Please try to be on time for everything. Acury runs on a strict schedule for very good reasons, after all! Now, let's learn something, shall we? Please switch on your computers."

Levi and the other kids all do as Sable says, but Levi frowns when he realizes how slowly the computer is switching on. He bends down under the table to look at the light-made wiring and grumbles under his breath. Most of them are connected badly and inefficiently. Some aren't even plugged in to the computer properly.

Levi crawls under, his byt curiously following, but not blaring anything. To Levi, that means he's probably not in trouble for breaking that silly schedule.

"Why would you connect a red to a blue?" Levi mutters under his breath as he starts working on the computer.

From the corner, Juniper is watching this new kid fiddling with the computer. She knows he's going to be in trouble, but she doesn't say anything. The way he's rearranging the lights will make the computer far faster. He's smart.

"Excuse me." Sable pauses next to Levi, who is still working on the cables with so much focus that he is sticking out his tongue. Sable is smiling as he bends down. "That was not the instruction given."

"The computer is slow," Levi answers simply, without stopping what he's doing. "I'm making it faster."

"That was not the instruction you were given." Sable is very calm when he repeats himself, folding his hands over each other. "Please return to your seat, and follow the instructions you were given. Otherwise, you will be removed from training and scheduled for additional regulation readings."

Levi shivers when he thinks about that. The RRGG is one of the most boring books he's ever read in his life. There are far too many rules.

Reluctantly, he gets up from under the computer and sits in the seat again. Sable smiles and looks at Levi's byt. "Please ensure that he completes the training according to instruction, or we will have to send you for correction."

Levi wonders what that means, but it's almost like his byt is nervous.

Chapter 3:

Noticing Talent

That night, Juniper thinks about the set of new colonists. Levi Helix was the only one that stood out to her. He's clearly talented and frustrated with all of the new rules, just like she is. She decides that she's going to be watching him a lot more carefully the next day, and goes to sleep hoping that Levi will keep up his spirits.

In the morning, Juniper goes to training again, full of anticipation. Today, they're supposed to teach the new colonists how credits work and how they can use them in the city. It's not exactly exciting, but it's considered crucial information.

At the training center, Levi is on time with all of the other new colonists. He sits behind his computer with his cheeks puffed up and a frown on his forehead.

That makes Juniper happy. Clearly he's still frustrated, and it looks like he doesn't plan on giving up.

Levi, meanwhile, feels like he could shake his surveillance byt. He's wondering if he could hack it, maybe change the alarm to something a bit more pleasant. They learned only how to log in and check in to all of Acury's systems the previous day—something he could have figured out himself.

Today, they're supposed to learn about credits, the city's money. But Levi doesn't care about that very much. After all, he's a kid. They can't expect him to work to earn any money, so he doesn't even know where he'll get it.

This time, though, Levi will be more careful. He will be behind the computer the whole time, and nobody's going to notice what he's doing. His plan is to explore Acury's networks while making the trainers think that he's only practicing spending credits... or whatever it is that they're planning to teach the new colonists.

"Step one." Sable starts wandering between the kids, watching their screens closely. "Log in, of course. Everyone, on three. One, two, fifty-five—"

He stops, laughing at the one kid who logged in on the third number. "I said on three. Let's start again."

Juniper wants to roll her eyes, but as a trainer, she can't. She goes to stand behind Levi to make Sable think that she's trying to make sure he's not deviating. But that's not what she wants. Juniper wants Levi to have a little bit of space to experiment—to prove how talented he is.

But of course, Levi doesn't know that. He thinks that the girl is monitoring him like the annoying byt does, to make sure that he doesn't do anything he shouldn't. Levi, however, is a clever kid, and he already has a plan. He's noticed that her byt sits on her shoulder like they're buddies.

So now, Levi is giving his byt little head scratches, wondering if that will work. It has done something. His byt goes to sit on his head, limiting its vision of his hands. He also shifts in his seat so that Juniper can't see his whole screen.

"Step two, open the credit app!" Sable announces, and everyone clicks at once, including Levi. But he clicks twice: once to open the app, and once to open its context menu. That's where he can find the console and a bunch of other codes that give information about the site. Being sneaky, he starts reading through it, looking for spots where he can change it.

Levi isn't as sneaky as he thinks. Juniper can see exactly what he's doing, and she's trying not to laugh. He's leaning so close to his screen with his tongue sticking out to the side of his mouth.

Luckily Sable isn't paying too much attention to Levi. He's still explaining the steps to accessing credits, and all of the other kids are following instructions closely. Juniper has her eyes glued to Levi's screen.

"Shutting down to charge battery," Levi's byt announces loudly. "Back-up byt necessary. Please clarify back-up byt code name."

Juniper glances at Sable before loudly announcing her own byt's name. "Byt code name Fly Billy, activate Back-Up Mode."

"Back-Up Mode activated," Fly Billy replies, hovering between Juniper and Levi. This makes Levi a little more nervous. He's hoping that Fly Billy won't see that he's trying to figure out how the whole network of Acury is put together.

For the whole training session, Juniper watches Levi closely. She's impressed enough that she makes a decision after training. She has a scheduled bathroom break, so she heads to one of the bathrooms close to the Trainers' Building where the byt's audio signals will glitch.

She hurries into a stall and gets out her very secret digital communicating device, called a Sectal, listening to make sure that nobody else is in the bathroom with her. Once she's sure, she uses her encrypted codes to call the Anonymous Adult.

The Sectal plays a little tune while Juniper waits, another way to keep it secret. If someone walks in now, they'll just think Juniper is listening to music on her break.

Finally, it crackles, and the Anonymous Adult's digitally changed voice comes through. "Code Name July, are you solo?"

Juniper sputters with laughter and holds her hand over her mouth, trying not to laugh too loudly.

"Uhm, Sir," she starts, shaking her head. "Sir, your voice changer makes you sound like a chipmunk."

The Anonymous Adult clears his throat, which comes out as a weird squeak, and there's a pause while he fiddles with something. When he speaks again, his voice is very deep. He pretends that nothing embarrassing has happened and repeats himself.

"Do you fly solo, Code Name July?"

"I do, Sir," she replies, turning serious again. "I have a report on a potential new recruit, Sir."

"You need to say that in code," the Anonymous Adult says with a sigh. Juniper wants to grumble under her breath. He always wants everything to be in code, no matter what it is. But Juniper thinks that's a little ridiculous. Nobody can hear her, and it would be a waste of time to constantly try to decipher the conversation.

"I'd like to talk about a new bird flying the coop," Juniper says anyway, knowing that the Anonymous Adult won't discuss anything unless she uses the code as he's asked.

"Good, excellent," the Anonymous Adult replies, and Juniper can imagine him rubbing his hands together. "From the new chicks, I imagine?"

"Yes, Sir," Juniper replies, trying to figure out how to explain things. "This bird isn't afraid to break the rules of the nest and he's good. His wings are strong."

"What?" the Anonymous Adult asks, completely confused, and Juniper puts her palm against her forehead.

"Sir, he's a smart kid and he hates the rules," she repeats with a grumble. "I want to ask permission to... I don't know how to make this a code. I want to ask him to join the revolution."

"Fine, fine, we'll talk normally, for now." The Anonymous Adult is obviously disappointed. He really likes keeping secrets and seeming like a cool spy. "Do you think that he's ready?"

"Either that, or he'll be kicked off the planet." Juniper shrugs, wiggling her toes. "He's definitely going to get himself in some real trouble if he doesn't learn to be stealthy."

"Hmm." The Anonymous Adult is quiet for a few seconds. "Then I suppose we—"

"Scheduled bathroom break is due to... to... to end in... one minute," Fly Billy says from outside the door, struggling to get its audio to work. "One, one, one minute."

"I have to go," Juniper says to the Anonymous Adult. "They might investigate its glitching. I'll talk to the new bird."

She ends the call and flushes the toilet, pretending that she's been using the bathroom like usual. Then, Juniper hurries out of the bathroom so that no one will notice that something is wrong with Fly Billy.

Now, all she needs to do is talk to Levi Helix and convince him to help win Acury's freedom.

Chapter 4:

A Fantastic Offer

For the rest of the day, Levi follows the rules closely. He's surprised that no one caught him during training, but he's not going to worry about that too much. That evening, Levi pretends to read the RRGG then goes to bed exactly on schedule. He's already wondering if he shouldn't do something drastic so that they'll send him back to Emberia.

Even if it doesn't have Acury's technology, he could at least work as a scientist there, maybe discover some new planets.

Levi rolls around in his bed, trying to fall asleep. The bed is specifically and perfectly made for him to be comfortable, but tonight, he just can't. He's thinking of ways to hack his own byt and whether it has a code name like Juniper's does. He's not sure how to even ask or how to activate different modes, because they haven't been taught any of that yet.

He wonders if the byt will sound an alarm if he tries to tamper with it. Or maybe, if it doesn't do that, someone will know that it's been tampered with and Levi will be in trouble.

Levi sighs as he rolls again, facing away from the digital window that's showing a pretty forest scene.

Suddenly, there's a sound behind him like the window is glitching and breaking apart. Levi jumps right out of the bed, holding up his fists like he's prepared to fight. He's never fought anyone before, but he has seen one kid punch another one. It doesn't look that difficult.

The person who appears through the window is wearing dark clothes with a hood. It's Juniper, who zips past the stunned Levi to shut down his byt with a few buttons. Her own is asleep and charging on her shoulder. Then she turns and lifts her hood over her head, shaking her messy lilac hair loose.

Levi stares at her, completely stunned.

"What's the matter?" Juniper asks with a grin, putting her hands on her hips. "Byt got your tongue?"

"Uh, I... Look... Uh..." Levi stutters. "Aren't you the trainer? I don't have any training scheduled..."

"You really think I'd break into your apartment in the middle of the night for scheduled training?" Juniper asks with one eyebrow raised. "Oh boy, I really thought you were a smart one. Maybe I was wrong."

"I am smart," Levi complains as he crosses his arms over his chest. "But even the cleverest people would be surprised if someone broke into their home in the middle of the night."

"A fair point," Juniper replies as she sits down on the edge of Levi's bed. "Unfortunately, I can't really talk to you about this during the day. It's a bit of a... secret."

She whispers the last word, making Levi curious. He's barely spoken to Juniper before, and so far she's only been monitoring him during training. Levi wonders if she's realized what he's been doing and is going to threaten to tell the adults. He hopes not. He's almost gotten into the programs that run the credit website.

"I've been watching you," Juniper says from the bed, crossing her legs and leaning forward with her hands on her knees. "You've been breaking a few rules, haven't you?"

Levi scratches at his head and lets his long fringe fall over both eyes, embarrassed and worried at the same time.

"The rules are stupid," he mutters, hoping that his byt hasn't heard him say that. "Who needs a schedule to go to the bathroom?"

Juniper laughs softly, making sure that she doesn't get loud enough to reactivate either of the byts. They only have a short amount of time to have this whole conversation anyway. Hopefully all of the monitoring officials are asleep in their chairs and haven't noticed that two byts have gone offline.

"A lot of people actually agree with that," Juniper points out, her face turning serious. "That's why we've started the Anti-Rule Revolution."

"The what now?" Levi blinks at her a few times. That is absolutely not what he expected her to say.

"Anti-Rule Revolution," Juniper repeats very slowly, taking a deep breath. "We are working to set everyone on Acury free from the schedules, the rules, all of the nonsense that's keeping us trapped."

Levi raises an eyebrow, immediately intrigued. "Really? Why are you telling me this, though?"

"Because I've seen what you've been doing in training," Juniper answers, jumping up from the bed to put her hand on Levi's shoulder. "You're talented and have potential. Frankly, it's impressive."

Levi turns red, looking at the floor. "Shucks, thank you."

Then, he pauses and realizes that Juniper really has known about everything he's been trying to be sneaky about.

"So... You saw everything, then?" he sighs, his shoulders drooping. "I thought I was hiding it well enough."

Juniper grins at him and shakes her head. "I'm sorry, but you're about as stealthy as a neon sign. At least we can teach you how to improve that particular skill. And, of course, all of the others. You're talented, but not perfect. If Sable wanted to, he could trace everything you did on that computer, and you'd be in a ton of trouble."

This time, Levi turns pale. "You think he will?"

"Don't worry," Juniper answers, letting go of Levi's shoulder and taking a step back. "The Revolution has already taken care of that for you."

Relieved, Levi sinks back against the wall. He's sure that they didn't do it for free, though. Juniper has to be here because she wants something from him. But what is it? He hopes that she'll get to the point soon. He's exhausted, and the schedule will make him get up incredibly early in the morning again.

"In fact, I have been sent here to recruit you into our ranks," Juniper explains with a wide smile. "The Anonymous Adult thinks that you'll be able to make a big difference for us."

"The who now?" Levi frowns. He's never heard of this person, but he supposes that makes sense. With a code name like "the Anonymous Adult," nobody likely knows who they really are in the first place. Seems like an incredibly secretive person who's much more successful at being sneaky than Levi.

"Look." Juniper puts her hands together in front of her face. "There's a revolution. We want you to join it. You'll get to learn how to hack secretly and how to hide what you're doing. You'll get to help to win Acury's freedom from all the rules and schedules. You'll get to see and work in our headquarters. That's what I'm offering. You can take it or leave it, but if you do leave it, we'll watch you very closely to make sure you don't say anything to anyone."

Levi thinks about it. He knows that this is the perfect opportunity to do what he really wants to do, but he also knows he'll probably still get a lot of orders to do what they want him to do.

Still, it's so much better than not doing anything at all and just following these ridiculous rules forever. If he can win his freedom, and freedom for the rest of Acury, then maybe he can fulfill his dream of becoming the galaxy's best digital inventor.

"Okay, I'll do it!" Levi grins, clapping his hands together. "When do we start? Right now?"

"Whoa," Juniper laughs, shaking her head. "Don't worry, we'll tell you. For now, we'll reactivate our byts and you'll go to bed. Pretend like you don't know anything and follow the rules *exactly* tomorrow. We don't want anyone to get suspicious, do we?"

"Yeah, fine." Levi sighs. His excitement has been dulled a little, but he still doesn't think he'll be able to sleep after all of this. He can't wait to see what happens in the morning.

Juniper fiddles with Levi's byt for a minute before disappearing through the window again. Levi watches her go, waiting for his byt to yell at him and ask why he's out of bed.

"You are scheduled for sleep," his byt starts up, the alarm wailing through the room. "Please return to bed."

Levi rolls his eyes. "Okay, okay, I'm going! Relax."

Chapter 5:

Hacking Heaven

Just like Levi thought, he struggles to fall asleep again, though he stays in bed with his eyes closed so that the byt doesn't start yelling at him. He wonders how Juniper switched it off so easily and whether she can teach him the same thing.

The next day, Levi follows the rules as closely as possible, even when he is bored out of his mind with training. At least they've finally learned what their byts are called. Levi's is called Beetle Bob, a name that doesn't really fit, but it doesn't seem to mind. Levi slogs through the rest of training, through dinner, and through his shower. It's been incredibly difficult, waiting for night to come.

Levi has been thinking about the Anti-Rule Revolution all day. How many people are part of it? Where are their headquarters? How come they haven't been caught yet? What happens to the byts while they're at the headquarters? There are a million more questions that Levi desperately wants to ask.

He rolls over in his bed, putting his hands under his head. It's late and incredibly dark outside. Maybe Juniper won't come tonight at all. She could have thought it would be funny to prank him, and the whole thing has just been one big joke.

However, while Levi is thinking that, Juniper suddenly appears through his window once again. She grabs his byt before it can raise the alarm and switches it off. Levi still wants to know how to do that.

"Right, come on, we have to go quickly before someone sees us," Juniper says, placing Beetle Bob in Levi's hand and leading him to the window. Levi wonders why he has to take his byt along, but he doesn't question it. Surely Juniper knows what she's doing, and besides, Levi is far too excited about everything new that's going on to ask.

Juniper glitches the window and helps Levi out onto a platform, which zooms through the city faster than any he's been on before. They go so fast that his cheeks fill up with air and his hair whips out behind his head.

"There," Juniper shouts, so loudly that Levi is nervous she'll wake up the entire city. "You see that dark spot?"

The platform slows, and Levi looks down to where Juniper is pointing. In the corner of a random street, there's a small, squat building that's slightly less bright than any of the buildings around it. It seems to flicker in and out of existence, like there's something wrong with its programming.

It's not very impressive, so much so that Levi wonders if it can really even be called a headquarters of anything. But he doesn't say that out loud while the platform hovers down onto the street and releases them.

"I know it doesn't look like much." Juniper shrugs as she steps forward across the sidewalk. "Just trust me, though. The inside is going to blow your mind."

She leads Levi up to the door before tapping their surveillance byts a few times. Both wake up and hover above Levi and Juniper's shoulders.

"Wait a minute," Levi complains, suddenly frozen. "They can't come with us; they'll see that we're breaking the rules and... the alarms!"

He puts his hands over his ears, expecting Beetle Bob to start screaming any moment. To Levi's surprise, both surveillance byts are completely silent. He blinks a few times and turns red when Juniper starts to chuckle at him.

"They don't work like they should around this building," she explains as she starts typing codes into the door. "None of us really know why, but it's incredibly convenient and useful. Don't worry, nobody will realize that we were here at all. As far as the Monitors are aware, you're still sleeping soundly in your bed."

"Oh," Lucas replies, dropping his hands from his ears and feeling rather silly. "I didn't know that."

Juniper looks back to grin at him as the door to the headquarters slides open. Lucas can see neon lights on the other side, and his heart starts beating faster from excitement. He's finally going to be able to do what he's been dreaming of his whole life. Maybe here, he can find the freedom that he thought he'd get on Acury.

They step into a gloomy hallway with dozens of doors leading into other rooms. Here, there are dim purple lights running along the ceiling. The other rooms flash with different colors at various levels of brightness. Juniper walks past most of them, but Levi can't help sneaking a peek into each one.

He sees several computers in most of them, along with other flashing devices and gadgets that he doesn't recognize. There are a few people wearing dark sweatshirts and looking sneaky, too, but they're actually good at it. Levi doesn't see any of their faces at all. He wonders if he's seen them around the city or at training. If he has~~did~~, none of them ever seemed suspicious.

Eventually, Juniper takes Lucas into a big lounge that almost looks like an arcade. There are antique game machines along the walls, huge couches and bean bags, several vending machines ~~along the walls~~, and a few old computers in the corner. There are three people in this room: one girl and two boys, each wearing the same hooded sweatshirt.

They, however, are hanging out on the couches with their faces very much visible.

"This is it," Juniper announces to Levi with her arms outstretched. "Where all the magic happens."

Levi's jaw hangs as he tries to take it all in. There are a whole bunch of neon lights against the wall, making this room brighter than any of the others in the building. The people on the couch are curiously staring at him, though most of them are wearing smiles. They look only a few years older than Levi, around the same age as Juniper.

"This is Belle, Art, and Hank," Juniper announces, pointing to each of them in turn. "They report to me. Naturally, you will report to them *and* to me, because I'm the one who recruited you."

Levi nods, waving awkwardly at the gathering of teenagers. Art and Hank both smile at him and nod, but Belle grumpily looks away like she's angry at the whole world.

"Of course, the Anonymous Adult runs the whole operation," Juniper continues with a sigh. She wishes that she was the one in charge, but she simply doesn't have the kind of high-level access and networking that the Anonymous Adult does. "You'll never meet him. He really likes staying hidden and being a big mysterious secret person."

Belle, Art, and Hank all nod at that, but Art is the one who speaks. "None of us have met him, and he only talks to Juniper."

"Sometimes we wonder if she didn't just make him up," Hank adds with a wink and a laugh. Juniper glares at him, but he doesn't pay any attention to him. "Doesn't matter, anyway. We're going to set Acury free."

"How?" Levi asks, still in awe at this whole thing.

Juniper waves her arms at the room around them. "Using computers, of course. We get orders from the Anonymous Adult, and then we do as he says. We've hacked into most of the digital networks in the city already."

"Not security," Belle mumbles. "We haven't gotten into security yet."

"We will," Juniper insists in return. Levi senses tension between the two of them. They probably get into a lot of arguments. "Just got to keep trying. Soon, we'll get into all of the byts, including the council's. Sable is never going to see that coming. And you, Levi, get to be a part of our Revolution."

Levi grins, unable to help himself. "This is the best day of my life!"

Chapter 6:

Don't Get Caught

Juniper takes Levi to one of the computers, and he sits down, excited to get started.

"We can only stay here for an hour tonight," Juniper explains, glancing at the byt on her shoulder. "I'll let you figure out the systems alone. I have my own orders to follow. Ask the others if you have any questions."

Now, Levi is really bursting with excitement. Once Juniper walks away, he bounces in his seat a few times to celebrate. He's so happy that nobody is going to be looking over his shoulder and making him follow the rules. He finally has the chance to explore everything behind the scenes of Acury's digital networks. It's a dream come true.

He switches on the computer, but impatience quickly sets in. This one takes even longer than the ones in the training center. They're much older than any of the computers Levi has ever seen in his life. He wonders if he'll even be able to work on them at all.

"Come on, come on," Levi grumbles when it takes longer than a minute for the first screen to pop up. When it does, he's even more frustrated. He is so impatient that he taps both of his feet at the same time. Finally, the screen lights up with what looks like a search bar. It has two words above it.

"Secret passcode," Levi reads aloud and frowns. Nobody has given him a secret code of any kind at this point. He looks over his shoulder. "Uh, how do I get in?"

Art gets up from the couch, stretching himself out. "That's a test. You have to figure it out yourself."

All three of them leave, and Levi is alone, staring at a screen that makes no sense at all. He stares and stares some more. Eventually the words start to blur, but nothing seems to jump out at him. Eventually, he decides that he's going to try something, even if it is completely and utterly ridiculous.

Secret passcode, Levi types into the bar, and the screen changes.

"Congratulations, and welcome to the Anti-Rule Revolution," the text flashes in bright colors, playing a little song in the background. Levi's jaw drops in surprise. He can't believe that the test was that simple. It doesn't seem very secure or secret to him at all.

"Your first step is to learn the map of the city and all of the digital devices within it by heart," the screen reads before loading a detailed and complex map. Levi stares at it, slightly disappointed. "Ah, man, more studying? Haven't I already been punished enough?"

He sighs, but zooms in on the map anyway so that he can see the streets and the marked devices better. It's just as boring as he imagined, but at least nobody is monitoring him and yelling at him for breaking the schedule or the rules.

By the end of the hour, Levi has only managed to memorize the devices and location of about five streets.

Juniper pops into the lounge cheerfully and taps him on the shoulder. "Time to go. People are going to start getting suspicious. If we stay longer, they'll notice how badly our byts are malfunctioning."

Levi yawns and stretches himself out from his seat. "Are we coming back tomorrow?"

"Oh, yes, of course," Juniper nods, pretending to be very serious. "Tomorrow, and the night after that, and the night after that... You know, until the whole of Acury is free!"

Levi smiles. Maybe it will be worth living on this strict, rule-bound planet after all. Once everyone has their freedom, Levi will be able to invent whatever he wants, whenever he wants, with nobody standing over his shoulder.

Juniper leads him out of the headquarters and takes him back to his own apartment, where she fixes his byt and disappears into the night.

"Why are you awake?" Beetle Bob says immediately once it is properly back online. "Scheduled wake-up time is at 06:30. There are no scheduled bathroom breaks before wake-up time. Please return to bed immediately."

"Yeah, yeah," Levi says, getting under the covers. He's more tired than he expected, so this time, it's not that hard to do as the byt commands.

In the morning, Levi leaps up at the first sound of the alarm. He rushes through his morning schedule, already excited about going back to the headquarters that night. Beetle Bob is barely able to keep up announcing what's next on the schedule before Levi has already done it.

At training, Levi is being watched by Sable rather than Juniper, who must be busy with something else, since she doesn't even show up. Levi remembers that she told him not to get in trouble, and he plans to follow instructions to the letter.

Unfortunately, doing that is incredibly boring. Several times, Levi finds himself yawning in the middle of one of Sable's explanations or being distracted by something on the wall.

Once, Sable comes to squeeze his shoulder. "You should pay attention, Mr. Helix. This information is important for you to live within the rules of Acury. After all, we want a well-disciplined society that runs like a machine on this planet."

"Sorry, Sir," Levi answers, trying not to sigh from his boredom and frustration. "I'm trying my best."

"Try harder," Sable says with a smile, but it is forced. Children who cannot listen to instructions make him terribly angry. It shouldn't be that hard. All they have to do is what they are told. They don't even have to think. That's a fairly easy thing to do, in his opinion.

Levi can't wait until the planet is free and Sable can't tell him what to do anymore. For now, he opens windows on the computer's browser and clicks everything that he has to. But when the Anti-Rule Revolution finally gets through into the mainframe of the system, the whole planet will be free.

Then Levi can make every single computer faster—so fast that people will be shocked. He'll turn his byt into a useful friend rather than a monitoring menace. Most of all, he'll be able to invent new gadgets and fun things that everyone will like.

"Stop daydreaming," Sable instructs from over Levi's shoulder, making him jump. "You will fall behind on your schedule."

"Sorry," Levi says again, trying to remember what it is they're supposed to be doing.

Luckily, after training, they have a lunch break, and Sable is finally gone. Levi is so annoyed with him. Why does everything have to be so perfect? Levi can't understand it. The whole world won't go down in flames just because he daydreamed for a few minutes.

But Levi doesn't dwell on that for too long. After lunch, there's a study session, then another quick training session with a different trainer, and finally, dinner. It's not long before it's bedtime, and Levi waits with bated breath for Juniper to come and get him.

That night, Juniper shows him more of the headquarters. She teaches him how to activate and deactivate his own byt and how to sneak around the city without being seen. Levi has to spend another hour studying the map, and he gets a little further than last time.

Every night thereafter, for days and days on end, Levi leaves his room to go to the revolution headquarters. By day seven, he's so tired during training that he almost falls asleep.

Still, he knows it's going to be worth it. The planet will be free.

Chapter 7:

Odd Orders

Eight days into Levi's training, he and Juniper are the only ones at the headquarters. Most of the revolution members are exhausted and have taken the night off. Juniper, however, never takes time off. She's impressed to see how dedicated Levi is, too.

She's seen him during the day, half-asleep most of the time. But at night, when he's here, it's like he's an entirely different person. He's focused and driven: exactly the kind of person that the revolution needs.

"What am I doing tonight, Boss?" Levi asks excitedly as they walk into the building and to the lounge. "I know the map by heart now, so I can spy on people, right? I can hack into the mainframe and disrupt the system. Oh, or I can prank Sable. He deserves it."

Juniper crosses her arms firmly and rolls her eyes over her shoulder at Levi. "Absolutely not. We're supposed to stay under the radar."

"You're no fun," Levi pouts. "I don't want to study anymore. I want to do something *cool.*"

Juniper sighs as they reach the lounge. She agrees with him, but there's nothing they can do until the Anonymous Adult gives them new orders. He's been quiet for several days. Juniper hopes it's because he has some huge plan where they'll finally do important stuff. She doesn't want to do all of this in secret anymore.

The Anti-Rule Revolution started when Juniper arrived on Acury, and it's been three years. To her, that feels like forever. Nothing has really changed, except that they've gotten a headquarters and learned how to be sneaky.

"Okay, look," Juniper says to Levi now as she sinks into one of the very comfortable couches in the lounge. "Why don't you play a game while we wait, huh? Or mess around on one of the computers?"

Levi kicks at the floor with his foot, grumbling under his breath, but he does eventually walk away. Juniper is just as frustrated, but she pretends not to be. Showing emotions would make her look less cool. Or, at least, that's what she thinks.

She pulls her Sectal from her pocket and stares at the screen, the same thing she did the previous night. Her foot wants to tap impatiently, but she refuses to let it do so. The Anonymous Adult has never gone this long without contacting her, and it's really getting annoying.

A part of her wonders if he's been discovered and captured by the council. That would be pretty terrible. Juniper doesn't know if she could become the new leader of the Anti-Rule Revolution, but maybe she should. Things would finally start moving faster.

Suddenly, the Sectal begins to ring. Juniper gets such a fright that she drops it on the floor. She looks around, embarrassed, but Levi didn't see her. He's focused on the computer in front of him.

Juniper gets up from the couch and leaves the room to answer the call. "Where have you been? We haven't heard from you in days!"

"Code Name July, are you solo?" the Anonymous Adult replies, completely ignoring Juniper's questions. She sighs with frustration and rubs her forehead, knowing that she's not going to get an explanation.

"Yes, I am," Juniper confirms, walking into the first open room in the hallway. "What are your orders, Sir?"

"This is top-secret," the Anonymous Adult insists, making Juniper roll her eyes.

"They always are, Sir. You know I won't tell anyone, except those the orders are directed to."

"Excellent." This time, he sounds almost excited. Juniper wonders what his next plans are. So far, they've been mostly harmless and pretty boring. "Now, you know how I've taught you to trace surveillance bugs throughout the city?"

Juniper remembers. It's a long and tedious process, and it was very difficult to break into that network. A few weeks earlier, she finally managed it.

"Yes, Sir," she says, a tiny bit of hope in her tone. Maybe they'll finally get to do something worthwhile.

"I need you to hack into that network and track the byts of all of the planet council members," the Anonymous Adult orders, surprising Juniper completely. "I need you to make sure that we can see everything they're doing, at every minute of every day."

Juniper already has a question about that order. It's different from anything that the Anonymous Adult has ever told her to do.

"Why?"

"Haven't I told you before not to defy me?" This time, he sounds pretty annoyed, perhaps even angry. "How do you expect to destroy them all if we don't know where they are or what they're doing?"

Juniper has never thought about doing that to anyone, not even the planet council. They're all sticklers for the rules, sure, but she doesn't think that means they need to be destroyed.

"Uh, Sir, I—" she starts, but the Anonymous Adult interrupts her.

"Do you want your freedom or not?"

Juniper takes a deep breath. "I do, Sir."

"Then you will do as I say," he growls through the voice modulator. "Or else!"

The call ends, leaving Juniper to stare at the Sectal in confusion. The Anonymous Adult has always had an odd personality, but these orders are particularly strange. The way he talks about them is particularly weird. The whole thing gives Juniper an uncomfortable feeling in her gut.

She has to wonder if she's just crazy. Juniper decides that she'll give Levi some of these orders and see what he thinks. If he does them without question, Juniper will know that she's just letting her imagination run wild. But if Levi argues with them, then... Well, maybe there's more to the Anonymous Adult's intentions than simply setting the people of Acury free.

Juniper heads to the lounge with a frown on her face. "Levi?"

He doesn't hear her. He's got his tongue sticking out and his eyes glued to the screen in front of him. Juniper walks closer and taps Levi on the shoulder. He swings around on his chair with wide eyes and raised fists, ready to fight.

When he sees it's just Juniper, Levi blushes with embarrassment and lowers his hands. "Sorry. What, uh, what's up?"

Juniper wants to laugh about Levi trying to act cool, but she has important things to attend to. She has to be serious, for now.

"We've gotten new orders," she explains, and Levi's face lights up immediately. He's been waiting for this for what feels like forever. Levi does notice, however, that Juniper seems a bit concerned. He wonders what's wrong, even though he knows that she probably won't tell him anything personal.

"We're going to hack into the surveillance byt network," Juniper starts, and Levi leans forward in his seat. "And we're going to permanently track the planet council members from the headquarters. You'll take the first shift."

Immediately, Levi frowns, biting the inside of his mouth. He's not sure how this is going to help set anyone free. The council are the ones who track and spy on people. It seems like something the bad guys in a story would do.

"Uh, why?" he asks, confirming for Juniper that these orders really are weird. "We could just break all the byts at once, or wipe their surveillance programs. What do we need to stalk people for?"

"You're not supposed to ask questions." Juniper crosses her arms and speaks with a snappy tone, even though she's now suspicious of the Anonymous Adult herself. "You're supposed to do as I say. Don't you remember? You report to me."

Levi grumbles under his breath. He didn't join the Revolution just to have more rules. In fact, it's supposed to be the opposite.

"Are you going to do what I say, or not?"

Levi shrugs. "I guess so."

"Good, then be quiet and do it." Juniper goes to sit at the next computer, setting it up to start working on the Anonymous Adult's orders herself. But she's worried. What if the Revolution really aren't the good guys? What if the Anonymous Adult is planning something nefarious?

Chapter 8:

Actually a Bad Guy

By the time Juniper and Levi manage to get past the surveillance byts' security system, it's nearly morning, and both of them are completely exhausted. Juniper decides to call it a night, and they leave the headquarters.

Levi switches his byt back to its normal mode once he gets to his apartment and immediately crashes into bed. He's so tired he can barely keep his eyes open, so he falls asleep pretty quickly. His dreams are filled with code and surveillance byts, all angry at him for hacking into their systems.

He only gets to sleep for about two hours before he's woken up by Beetle Bob's incredibly loud alarm. Grumbling, Levi rolls out of bed and peers at the byt.

"You can't relax for even a second, can you?" Levi yawns, shaking his head to try and clear it.

Levi can't really pay attention or remember anything for most of the day. He falls asleep twice during training and almost lands face-first in his lunch. Several times, Levi gets sour looks from the other kids and the trainers. Sable in particular seems very suspicious, but since Levi's byt won't show any unusual activity, Levi doesn't think he'll get in trouble.

By the time dinner rolls around, Levi is completely exhausted. He can't wait to finish up the day and sleep for as long as Beetle Bob will allow him to.

He rushes through his meal and goes up to shower. To his surprise, the byt doesn't argue and insist he stay until scheduled dinner is finished. When Levi tries to go to bed before study hour, however, Beetle Bob bristles and whines.

"You are scheduled for a one-hour RRGG reading," the byt announces, buzzing around Levi's head. "You are not yet scheduled for sleep. Please follow the mandated schedule. There have already been two schedule violations on your record today."

Levi thinks about just switching Beetle Bob off now that he knows how. But it's still early in the evening, and no doubt the Monitors would notice that something is off if Levi does anything to his byt before scheduled bedtime. With a big, overdramatic sigh that the byt doesn't understand at all, Levi grabs his copy of the RRGG and pretends to read it.

He falls asleep with his face in between the pages, but Beetle Bob doesn't register that and doesn't send an alarm.

Levi is only woken up again when someone is shaking him by the shoulders. He blinks a few times and yawns, peering over his shoulder in the darkness of his apartment. Juniper is standing next to him. She's furiously glaring at him, even though neither of them can see each other that well.

"You're late," Juniper growls angrily. "I thought they caught you or something."

"What? Huh?" Levi stretches himself out. "What time is it? Where am I?"

"It's almost midnight!" Juniper snaps in a wild whisper, putting her hands on her hips. "You were supposed to be at the headquarters over an hour ago!"

"I'm sorry." Levi gets up from his seat, his whole body sore from sleeping in such an odd position. "I'm tired."

"The Revolution cannot rest!" Juniper replies immediately as she pumps her fist in the air. "If we want change, we can't take naps!"

Levi has no idea what she's talking about. She seems more riled up than usual.

"Okay, I'm coming," he says, following her to the window. "What are we supposed to do tonight? More weird stuff?"

Juniper doesn't answer. She's already worried about the Anonymous Adult's orders from the previous night, and she doesn't know if she trusts him anymore. But she's not going to say anything about it until she's sure.

She takes Levi down to the headquarters, where they head straight to the lounge. Levi is convinced that Juniper is angry with him for oversleeping and being late. He can't think of another reason for her to be so grumpy and quiet.

In the lounge, Belle, Art, and Hank are all sitting behind computers, furiously typing and clicking as if they're busy with something important. Belle is the only one who glances over her shoulder when

Juniper and Levi walk in. All she does is roll her eyes, scoff, and turn back to her screen. To Levi, that confirms that everyone is furious at him for sleeping when he should have been hacking.

"Did we get new orders, then?" Levi asks curiously, knowing that they already got into the surveillance byts the previous night.

Juniper shakes her head. "They're just tracking the council."

Before she can explain further, her Sectal rings, and she disappears from the room. Levi sinks into the couch, planning on just resting his eyes for a little while. After all, Juniper didn't actually give him anything to do. He might as well enjoy his break while he has the chance.

"Are you sleeping again?" Juniper's annoyed snap wakes Levi up nearly 15 minutes later, and he realizes that he's been snoring. "I swear, I can't leave you alone for one second. Why aren't you helping them? Can't make decisions on your own?"

This time, Levi doesn't think Juniper's attitude is from her being angry at him. "Are you okay?"

Juniper is pulled out of her frustration by that question and by how sincere Levi looks. She sighs and takes a glance at the others, who are all still deeply focused on their computers. In her mind, she makes a decision to trust Levi with her suspicions. He's the only one who thought the Anonymous Adult's orders were weird.

The others all started working on tracking the council without even a single question.

"Come with me," Juniper tells Levi before swinging around on her heels and marching out of the lounge. If the Anonymous Adult really is a bad guy, she doesn't want him to become suspicious of her. He might do something drastic to stop her from telling anyone else or getting in his way.

Juniper takes Levi into a broom closet and shuts the door behind him. It's the only place with no digital equipment inside that could possibly track them or eavesdrop on their conversation.

"Uh..." Levi looks around at the cleaning implements, most of which are ancient and probably not very useful on Acury. "I don't know what we're going to hack into next, but I don't think I could do it from here."

Juniper shakes her head and starts rummaging through everything to make sure there is absolutely nothing that could spy on them.

"You're scaring me," Levi says, wondering if he could escape through the door before Juniper can catch him.

"Okay, nobody's watching." Juniper heaves a sigh of relief and sits down on a box full of random things. "You need to listen to me. I need to figure out if I'm just going crazy."

Tentatively, Levi sits down on the floor across from her, close enough to the exit to escape quickly if he needs to. He peers at Juniper suspiciously, wondering what's going on in her head.

"I think the Anonymous Adult might be a bad guy," Juniper explains, leaning forward on her knees. "My gut feeling is telling me that he's up to no good, and we have to stop him."

Levi ponders what she's saying. He's not sure what's made her think all of this, but he's never trusted the Anonymous Adult himself. Mostly, Levi just doesn't trust adults at all.

"Why?" he asks, tapping at his chin. "Has he given you more weird orders?"

"He wants us to trap the council in their buildings." There's a deep concern on Juniper's face now. "He says it's so that we can complete the rest of the plan without interference, but I don't believe him. I think he wants to do something terrible."

Levi's eyes grow wide. "Yeah, that... that really doesn't sound good. We should... we should probably stop him, shouldn't we?"

"I think so."

Chapter 9:

Troubling Trouble

Finding time to try and uncover and foil the Anonymous Adult's plot in between training, being part of the Anti-Rule Revolution, and following the schedule is almost impossible for both Juniper and Levi. At most, they get a few minutes a night in the broom closet to talk about their suspicions.

They can't even try and look into the computers too much, because the Anonymous Adult is definitely tracking everything that they're doing. To both Levi and Juniper, it seems like they won't be able to do anything about the Anonymous Adult's true intentions in time to save... whatever it is they should be saving from him.

But that's not even the only problem they face. A few days after their first meeting in the closet, Juniper and Levi are in the lounge, pretending to follow orders, when the computer screens light up red.

Big, bold, capitalized words rush across them.

BREAKING NEWS: RULE-BREAKERS CAUGHT BREAKING RULES

Levi and Juniper look at each other with wide eyes before they turn back to the screens. Several pictures pop up, and they recognize every single person that appears. First, Belle, Art, and Hank. Then, all of the other members of the Anti-Rule Revolution. Everyone except for Juniper and Levi.

"Oh, no," Juniper whispers as a robotic voice starts to speak in the background of the breaking news announcement.

"Several members of a local rule-breaking cabal have been caught red-handed," the voice says, the pictures flashing across the screen again. "Their surveillance byts were instrumental in their apprehension. We urge the public to remain calm. These dangerous criminals are now in our custody and you have nothing to worry about. Remember to follow your schedules closely."

Juniper and Levi keep staring at the screens in absolute shock, even when they go blank.

In a building pretty far away from the headquarters, an anonymous shadowy figure is watching the same news with a sneer on his face. He knew that this was going to happen. He was a part of the reason for it. Finally, he knows that it is time for his grand plan to go into action. It's too bad two of the kids haven't been caught, but that doesn't matter. They're just children. They won't be able to do anything about it.

Meanwhile, back at the headquarters, Juniper and Levi turn to each other. Juniper swallows.

"We're in pretty big trouble now, aren't we?" she says, sitting back in her seat and putting her hands behind her head. "Do you think they'll tell the Monitors about us?"

Levi turns completely pale. He didn't even think about that. If the others are interrogated, they might tell the Monitors where the headquarters are and what they've been doing. Hopefully they won't say anything at all, but there's no guarantee of that.

"I don't know," Levi replies honestly, getting up from his chair. "But this place is probably going to be compromised no matter what, isn't it?"

Juniper leaps to her feet when she thinks about that. It's possible that the Monitors are on their way at that very moment. If they were, though, they probably would already be at the headquarters before they even broadcast the breaking news.

"We should talk to the Anonymous Adult," Juniper whispers, knowing that Levi might not agree. Juniper doesn't think that the Anonymous Adult is behind this, but if she and Levi don't report to him, they'll be in trouble. He's definitely seen the news already, and he might be waiting for communication.

Juniper pulls out her Sectal and stares at it. She can't really contact the Anonymous Adult. She has to wait for him to call her, usually. There's an emergency line, though, a messaging app that he told her never, ever to use unless the headquarters are on fire.

Now, the building hasn't gone up in flames, but Juniper is sure that the Anonymous Adult didn't actually mean any of that literally. The revolution itself is in trouble. Of course, Juniper still thinks the Anonymous Adult is up to something terrible, but she can't let him become suspicious of her and Levi. He needs to think that they're still completely loyal to him.

Luckily, or perhaps unluckily, Juniper's Sectal starts to ring before she can start typing a message.

Nervously, she answers the call, making sure that Levi can listen in to everything that's being said. Juniper places her finger over her mouth to tell him to be quiet. The Anonymous Adult can't know that Juniper isn't alone.

"Hello?" she says into the receiver, the tension in the room growing strong. "Sir, I can report that Littlest One and I are both safe inside headquarters."

Levi peers at her grumpily. He's had no idea that Littlest One is his codename. It sounds a bit mean, in his opinion.

"What happened?" The Anonymous Adult demands immediately. He sounds completely furious. "I told you that you cannot make any mistakes!"

"I didn't," Juniper points out truthfully. "I don't know how any of them got caught. We've all been incredibly careful."

"Did anyone follow you to the headquarters?" At this point, the Anonymous Adult is pretty close to shouting. Of course, he knows exactly how the others were caught. He tipped off the Monitors himself. It's all part of his grand plan. The only problem now is the two that are left. But they seem to be oblivious to his deviousness. They won't be able to do anything even if they do eventually figure it out.

"I don't think so." Juniper starts pacing around the room. "Littlest One and I are safe, for now. I'm not sure if they know where we are or what we're really doing."

"You clearly don't understand how much of a problem this is," the Anonymous Adult snaps back at her. "The two of you are all that is left. You'll have to work through the night, every night. Ten times faster and harder than you ever have."

That makes Juniper really worried. They've already barely had any time to investigate the Anonymous Adult as it is. If they can't even take a five-minute break at night and they barely get any sleep at all, that will make it so much harder to do anything at all.

"We could try to recruit more members, maybe—" Juniper starts, but the Anonymous Adult cuts her off in the middle of her sentence.

"Absolutely not!" he hisses, something that sounds very odd through the voice changer. "The Monitors are on hyper-alert for any suspicious activity. You cannot trust anyone at all. Do you understand me? You two are on your own. Now, do what you've been ordered, and don't go to bed until you have control of the locking mechanisms on the council's buildings!"

"Okay, okay," Juniper breathes, but the Anonymous Adult ends the call right there. She turns to Levi and mouths the words *broom closet*.

The two of them hurry out of the lounge and to their ultra-secret meeting spot, where Juniper checks for cameras again while Levi closes the door. Both of them are panicking and trying not to let the other one see.

"He's definitely evil," Levi points out the obvious. "Right? I mean, listening to him... It's obvious."

"I feel stupid for not seeing it earlier," Juniper says, sighing in agreement. "But what are we going to do now? We have to stop him, but we don't even know what he's planning. And we can't tell anyone else. They'll arrest us, and they won't believe us."

"Honestly, I don't know," Levi shrugs. "But we'll figure something out. We just have to."

Chapter 10:

A Surprising Identity

Just before the two of them decide to leave the broom closet, Levi gets an idea. "Wait."

Juniper turns around from where she's standing at the door, hoping that Levi will say something that could change this whole situation. Levi is grinning like an idiot with his hands on his knees.

"Could you find the Anonymous Adult's surveillance byt somehow?" he asks, making Juniper frown as she wonders if she could. "Maybe with the Sectal? It wouldn't be easy, obviously... but is it possible?"

Juniper paces around in the tiny space in front of Levi. "Perhaps. I mean, I think so. I could give it a try. Don't you think he'll notice?"

"If he does, we'll act dumb." Levi shrugs. He hasn't thought about that at all. Really, he's hoping that things will go their way for once. "But it's something, at least. We need to try, don't we?"

"Yeah, you're right." Juniper smiles as she puts her right fist in her left hand. "We're both smart. We can do this."

Neither of them are actually sure if they can, but that doesn't matter. They have to hold onto the hope of possibility.

"Okay, you do that, and I'll try and get into the buildings," Levi says, finally feeling a bit more enthusiastic about their situation. "That way we can pretend that we're still doing what he wants."

Juniper nods. "Right, yes, of course. Let's go before he calls again and starts asking questions."

The two of them leave the broom closet and go to sit at the computers. Juniper connects her Sectal and gets to work, while Levi accesses the blueprints of the city. There are four council buildings in different corners. While they're all connected to the same network, they're going to be far more difficult to get into than anything else.

"Whoa, the security on these is insane," Levi points out with a sigh. "It might take a while to get into even one of them."

"Take your time," Juniper replies, knowing that the Anonymous Adult could be listening in on their conversation. "We have to do this right. We can't get caught like the others were."

The two of them spend several hours on their projects, Levi working as slowly as he can, Juniper as fast as she can. Unfortunately, by an hour before the digital sun will rise, Levi has gotten into a building already, but Juniper is only halfway to finding the Anonymous Adult's surveillance byt.

Turns out the Sectal is a lot more encrypted than she thought. But she's sure now that she will find him and that they will be able to confirm his identity.

"We should go to bed." Levi yawns, sitting back in his chair. "Nothing bad will happen in a single day, will it?"

Juniper turns her head toward him and smiles, even though she's incredibly anxious that a lot of terrible things could happen before the next night.

"No, it won't. Let's go." She gets up and stretches herself out before disconnecting the Sectal. They leave the headquarters nervously, expecting to be taken into custody as soon as they go through the front door. However, nobody ambushes them or catches them at any point, and they're both easily able to go back to their apartments.

Unfortunately, neither of them sleep very well or very long before their byts wake them up with their incredibly annoying alarms. For the whole day, neither Juniper nor Levi are really able to focus on anything that they're doing. During lunch, Levi even accidentally pokes himself in the cheek with his fork, since his mind is on that night and their mission.

This time, he switches off his byt a little early in the evening, hoping no one will notice that he missed his mandatory RRGG manual reading. When he reaches the headquarters, he's alone, and he hopes that Juniper hasn't been caught. It would be pretty awful to have to do all of this alone.

"Okay, I've got this," Levi says to himself as he walks through the eerily quiet hallways. A lot of the lights in the headquarters have been shut off completely. Luckily, everything in the lounge is still on. Juniper must have been here already to do all of that. It makes sense. They want to be as hidden as possible, so why not go as dark as they can?

Levi logs in and starts working on getting into the second council building. This one is going to take several hours—more than any of the others. For some reason, it has a lot more security. Almost like the person inside is worried anyone else will see what they're hiding.

That makes Levi suspicious, but he needs Juniper to get into that surveillance byt to see if he's actually right.

"I'm here," Juniper announces from behind him after about an hour, out of breath and stressed to her limits. "Sorry, I... I took a nap."

Levi isn't angry at that. He's impressed. "How'd you do that without your byt screaming your ears off?"

"I have my ways." Juniper grins as she makes her way to the computer beside Levi. "Anyway, let's see if we can find him, huh? I'll teach you how to break the schedule later."

"Listen," Levi says, sitting aside so that Juniper can see his screen. "I don't think you have to search through too many more byts. I think you should take a look at this one, specifically."

Juniper's eyes grow wide, and her jaw hits the floor as she looks at the complex codes behind the security of the building that Levi is now working on.

"You think that's him?" she asks, and Levi nods grimly. "Okay, it's as good a shot as any. I'll see what I can do."

Juniper puts her headphones over her ears and leans up close to the computer, typing like a madwoman. If Levi is right, then they've found the Anonymous Adult, and they're one step closer to uncovering his evil plot.

Levi glances over at Juniper's computer every now and again while he continues to try and get into the building's security. This time, he does his best to work a little faster. If this really is the Anonymous Adult's building, then being able to hack it might be very helpful.

"Wait, I think I might have it," Juniper says after what feels like several hours. "Yeah, I'm in!"

Levi leaves what he's doing behind entirely, scrambling closer on his wheeled chair to see what Juniper is looking at. She's managed to get into the Anonymous Adult's surveillance byt. On the screen, pixels start clearing up to show a picture.

"You were right," Juniper breathes, surprise burning in her tone. "It's him. It really is him."

"Oh, no." Levi blinks a few times, taking in what this could possibly mean. "Isn't he in charge of the whole surveillance system?"

"He is." Juniper nods. "He's the head of security, the one who made most of the rules. He's the one who must have caught all of the others."

Levi's jaw hits the floor. "Doesn't that mean he could catch us if he wants to?"

"Yeah."

"So... If we stop following his orders..."

"He'll lock us up."

The two of them are silent as they watch the screen. On it, the Anonymous Adult is sitting behind his own computer in his bedroom, though they can't see what he's doing.

Levi is still trying to process this. The man who has made most of the rules—the one who took all of the people on Acury's freedom—is the one leading the revolution. This is the evidence that Juniper and Levi needed.

Now that they know, they really have to stop him.

"Sable," Juniper growls. "We're coming for you. I hope you're ready."

Chapter 11:

A Secret Plot

Juniper and Levi decide to go to bed earlier than usual. They need more rest if they're going to take down one of the most important people on Acury. Juniper makes sure that Levi is asleep before she goes to her own apartment.

However, Juniper can't sleep at all. When she lies down on her bed, all she can do is stare up at the ceiling and think. She knows that the two of them are in a lot of danger. If Sable starts suspecting anything, he could easily expose them as revolution members and get them locked up with the others.

Juniper doesn't want Levi to get in trouble. She's the one who recruited him, so he's her responsibility.

Maybe I can end all of this without him being involved, she thinks, rolling over to her side. *If I can stop Sable myself, then I can keep Levi safe.*

She decides that this can't wait. She has to stop Sable's plot right away, now that she knows who he is.

Juniper leaps out of bed, grabbing her byt to stop the alarm before it can even start. She's going to find Sable and end this whole thing herself. Finding the darkest clothes that she owns, Juniper forms a plan in her head.

The clothes don't really fit anymore, since they're from a few years ago, but they'll have to do. Juniper puts her own surveillance byt on charging mode on her shoulder. If something happens, Levi should be able to gain access to it and find her. Juniper hopes, however, that that won't happen at all.

"All right, I'm doing this," she tells herself as she stands by the window. In the distance, she can see the building that belongs to Sable. "You won't see me coming."

She slips out of her apartment and takes a platform down to the streets, making sure that nobody is watching her. Most people should be in bed, according to their schedules. Most people never break the rules, either, so Juniper isn't too worried.

One person that might be awake is Sable himself. That could be a problem, but Juniper already has a plan. When she reaches his building, she starts looking for the maintenance entrance. Levi had discovered it earlier while he was trying to hack the place, and that was the first door he managed to get into. It was also the only one that he got into, but that's besides the point.

Juniper keeps herself right up against the wall of the building as she searches for the door, which would make it impossible to spot her from above. She finally finds it and manages to open it easily, thanks to Levi's hard work.

Proud of herself and her friend, Juniper makes her way inside. It's so quiet that the silence itself makes her nervous. She can hear her feet, her heartbeat, and her own breathing. Most of the lights are off, but Juniper has studied the blueprints of all of the buildings in the city and she knows exactly where she's going.

She finds the elevator after some winding through the hallways and takes it all the way up to the penthouse. At this point, she's not entirely sure what she's going to do. She wants to record Sable saying something that will expose him, but she doesn't know yet how she can broadcast that to the whole planet.

When she steps off the elevator and into the large foyer of the penthouse, the lights are still off. Juniper doesn't think that Sable is asleep. Something is fishy here, but she decides to press on.

She walks through the doors into the lounge, scanning the place to try and see what might be going on.

Suddenly, the entrance slams closed behind her and the lights above her all flash on, blinding her and forcing her to shut her eyes for several seconds. Juniper hears someone start to clap their hands slowly, coming closer from the other side of the room.

"I'm going to assume you're here because you've discovered my little secret," Sable's voice says, confirming to Juniper even more that he has some kind of terrible plot going on. "Too bad for you."

Juniper squares herself up and opens her eyes, letting them get used to the bright light. "What are you talking about? It's over! I'm going to expose you, and everyone will know how evil you really are."

"Hmm, I don't think so." Sable laughs and clicks his fingers. Out of the blue, several byts fly through the room, each grabbing onto one of Juniper's limbs and holding her in place.

"Hey, what... What's going on?" she demands as her own byt flutters off her shoulder and grabs onto her hair. "Let me go!"

"I'm afraid I can't do that," Sable replies, nodding at the byts as he starts walking away. "You see, letting you go would throw a wrench into my plans. I don't plan on being stopped, so, you can't leave. Don't worry—I'll make sure you're fed and that you get enough rest."

"You can't do this," Juniper hisses. She tries to fight against the byts, but they easily drag her after Sable, who is heading toward what looks like a massive safe with really thick metal walls. Juniper feels her stomach drop. Surely he's not going to lock her up in there, is he?

"I can do whatever I want." Sable shrugs as he starts working on opening the safe. "The whole planet trusts me, and they don't know what's waiting for them. Your little revolution friends are all locked up, aside from one little boy who won't be able to do anything at all. What makes you think anyone can stop me now?"

The door to the safe swings open slowly on its metal hinges, and the byts pull Juniper inside despite her protests. Once they've thrown her in, the door closes and becomes clear, turning into a window through which Sable is sneering at her.

"Don't worry, it's not soundproof," Sable says, knocking on the glass. "You know, at the moment. If you decide to scream, I'll have to change that."

Juniper glares at him furiously, even though she feels pretty hopeless. "What do you actually want, huh? You set up all the rules and then promised us freedom. Was that all a lie? Why would you do something like that?"

"Because I want to conquer the planet, obviously." Sable rolls his eyes. "Why else? I am in control of all of the rules, and with the help of you lovely young children, I am now in control of nearly all of the devices in the city. Soon, I will run this whole place without needing the rest of the council, and I will be well on my way to taking over the entire galaxy!"

Sable starts laughing, something he clearly practiced a lot to get just right. Unfortunately for him, he starts to cough in the middle of it, and has to pause to catch his breath again.

"Anyway!" he says, pretending that he's not embarrassed. "You will get to see the rest of my plan unfold from in there. Maybe you can stay there forever. We'll see."

Juniper has no idea how she can get out of this situation. Hopefully Levi will notice that something's wrong. At least he can still access her surveillance byt. All she can do now is to trust him and hope for the best.

"Oh, yes," Sable says as he grabs Juniper's byt out from among the rest, "I should probably switch this off. Pesky things tend to track movement. I wouldn't want anyone coming after you, now, would I?"

Chapter 12:

The Lonely Leader

None the wiser, Levi sleeps right through to the next day. He only realizes that something is wrong when Juniper doesn't show up for training at all, and Sable watches him far more closely than any of the other kids.

Levi continues to pretend like he's not suspicious of anything, like he has no idea about Sable's true identity. On the inside, though, Levi is very worried. He doesn't hear anything from Juniper all day, and he quickly becomes convinced that she must be missing.

That has to mean that the headquarters is compromised, Levi thinks to himself at lunch, trying to look like he's having a good day and following the schedule as he should. *I'm sure Sable has caught her, somehow.*

Levi decides that he won't go to the headquarters that night. He's certain that Sable will lay a trap and catch him, just like he's done with everyone else. Luckily, Levi has paid extra attention to the map of the city recently.

There's one corner that seems to glitch every time he attempts to load it. To Levi, that seems like a possible place for him to hide, where neither the Monitors nor Sable will be able to find him. Even if he does take his surveillance byt with him, he's sure he can remain hidden. Besides, Levi doesn't want to be completely alone.

Beetle Bob might be a weird little spy bug, but at least he's company.

The afternoon creeps by so slowly that Levi feels like he's going to lose his mind. Sable is still watching him uncomfortably closely, even coming to training sessions that he's not scheduled for. Levi is constantly worried that Sable will simply capture him and tell everyone that Levi is part of the revolution, but he doesn't.

What Levi doesn't know is that Sable is convinced the little boy is far too scared to do anything by himself. Besides, Sable is sure that this kid can't be smart enough to do much, even if he tries. The boy does nothing to make Sable think that he will try to save Juniper or any of the other members of the revolution. Frankly, Sable is not too worried by the time dinner rolls around, and he decides to ignore Levi to focus on his plan.

Levi, however, is still completely stressed out about what's waiting for him that night, especially after he switches off his surveillance byt when it is bedtime.

"I hope that Sable doesn't see this," Levi says when Beetle Bob goes to sleep. "Maybe he's too busy plotting. That would be the best, wouldn't it?"

Beetle Bob doesn't answer, obviously. Levi sighs as he puts the byt in his pocket. He doesn't think that he's ever felt as lonely as he does now.

Juniper taught Levi how to get through the digital window, but he still wishes that she was here to do it. But she would tell him to be brave and that he can do this. Levi takes a deep breath and opens the window, calling up a platform. Before getting on and leaving, he switches off its lights.

After all, it would be very suspicious if a bright platform soared through the city just after bedtime. Sable would definitely see it from his skyscraper.

Levi steers the platform as close to the ground and the buildings around him as he can. He feels pretty self-conscious in his silver pajamas. Any kind of light would bounce against them and light him up like a neon sign. He wishes he had darker clothes, but he got rid of everything he owned when he got here.

"We're almost there," Levi whispers, just to break the silence that's around him. His heart is beating very fast, and he can hear it in his ears. He hasn't been this nervous before in his life.

The glitch is at the far corner of the city, a tiny building that looks like it was supposed to be an arcade. Its neon signs' pixels are mostly broken, and Levi can't even make out the letters on them. In his pocket, Beetle Bob starts to vibrate as soon as the platform lands next to the glitched area, almost like the byt is shivering.

Levi feels a little bad about that, but he doesn't have a choice. This is the only place that Sable won't be able to find him, at least with digital means.

It's a bit creepy when Levi walks up to the building. Nothing works quite like it should. His hand goes through the doorknob, but when he turns it in the air, the door does open, jumping side-to-side as it glitches.

"This is weird," Levi says to himself and to Beetle Bob, who has stopped vibrating. Levi heads inside, where there are chairs on the roof, computers on the floor, and an old arcade game laying horizontally against one wall. At least the couch is on the ground, even if half of it is inside the next door.

"Okay, focus," Levi mumbles, trying not to be distracted by all of the strange things around him. "I have to see if one of these computers can actually work."

He tries switching on a few, but two of them just make a screeching noise. A third does switch on, but its whole screen is upside down. Luckily, the fourth one that Levi tests seems to work well enough, even if it is incredibly slow. Levi pulls a chair from the roof, using all of his strength, and picks up the computer to place it on a desk that's in a weird position in the corner.

It takes a lot of huffing and puffing and sweating, but Levi finally has his station set up and he's ready to log in. Impatiently, he taps his foot on the floor as the computer loads past the various screens. It struggles, making awful noises, but it eventually shows an interface screen that Levi can actually use.

"Right, Juniper. Where are you?" Levi asks as he locks his fingers together and stretches out his arms. He's ready for this, even if he's just one kid. He knows that he can take Sable down if he does his best.

Having already found the council's surveillance byts, Levi remembers everything that he did to get into them. All he has to do is to locate Juniper's byt and hack into the camera. That will tell him exactly where she is.

Levi leans in close to the computer and starts typing. First, he needs to get into the byt network. It's hard, but he's practiced a lot. It takes three screens before he gets to the password, which Juniper worked out. Levi notices now that the password is the same as Sable's byt's name.

He shakes his head. He has to focus. It might be a good idea to find Sable, too, but he'll do that after he gets a hold of Juniper. All Levi wants to know is that she's safe.

"Wait, there..." Levi peers closer at the screen. He's sure that's Juniper's byt on the list. But his eyes grow wide, and his heart drops as he reads its status.

OFFLINE.

Chapter 13:

A Gadget Revolution

The status of Juniper's byt convinces Levi that Sable did capture her. He checks all of the other revolution members' byts, too. Theirs say simply *Incarcerated*, which is different entirely. That means that Juniper is being held somewhere else.

"But where?" Levi mumbles to himself, smacking his forehead with his palm. "Think, Levi, think!"

That's when he gets a completely crazy idea—something that's wild and stupid and could get him in a whole lot of trouble. Still, if it works, he'll be able to find Juniper and maybe even save her. He could set everyone free.

All he has to do is implement this ridiculous plan absolutely perfectly, without making any mistakes at all. That's easy enough, isn't it?

Levi takes a deep breath and blows out all of the air in his lungs, trying to calm his nerves. He can definitely do this, even if he's never done anything even close to it before.

First, I need to control the byt network, he thinks, stretching his arms and cracking his neck. This might turn into a long night, but he doesn't mind. It's time for all of this to be over, and for Acury to finally be free from all the stupid rules Sable has made.

And, of course, for Sable's plot, whatever it is, to be stopped in its tracks.

Levi pulls Beetle Bob out of his pocket and places him on the desk. It makes him feel a little less alone to have his byt with him. Maybe, when Levi's plan succeeds, he can turn them into friends rather than foes.

Levi gets to work. Before, when they hacked into the surveillance byts' cameras, they could only see their statuses. Now, Levi has to try to hack into their command centers so that he can take control. He tries a few things, like the console command on the main site and the settings option in the menu.

But neither of those work. Of course not. Sable is evil, but he's smart, too. He wouldn't make it that easy to get into his systems.

Levi tries a fancier method, where he has to enter some complex codes to try and get to the source of how the byts work. With every minute that passes, he becomes more anxious, but he won't give up. Juniper wouldn't, if she was in his shoes. Besides, this is the right thing to do; Levi is sure of it.

"Wait just a minute." Levi grins as he spots something on the screen. "I think, maybe..."

He sticks out his tongue as his fingers fly across the keys of the computer. It takes some time, but Levi finally makes it onto a screen that looks like it will lead him in the right direction. Unfortunately, this one also wants a password.

Levi taps at his chin, wondering what kind of password Sable would use for this. It has to be something incredibly secure that nobody would guess. It can't be the name of his surveillance byt. It has to be something that is really important to him. But what is important to Sable?

"Rules?" Levi types the word in, but the screen shivers and tells him that he's wrong. "Sable himself?"

Wrong again. The screen lets him know that he has one more try before the whole system will be shut down and the alarms will be set off. That's not good.

Levi sits back in his chair and closes his eyes. At first, he can't think of anything at all. He hasn't exactly spent any time trying to figure out what makes Sable tick. Maybe he should have, but he's never thought that Sable is a particularly interesting person.

"Oh, wait." Levi laughs when he has another idea. It might be completely stupid, but Sable does like secrets and secret identities. Levi would bet that Sable really loves that nobody knows what's going on in his head.

Anonymous, Levi types in, and the screen flashes green, allowing him into the main network that controls every surveillance byt on the planet.

Levi leaps out of his chair and pumps his fists in the air a few times to celebrate. He's done it without anyone finding out. Well, he's completed step one of the plan. Now he needs a step two, and maybe a step three as well.

After his little victory dance, Levi sits down at the computer again and pets Beetle Bob on the head.

"Let's see if I can get all of their alarms shut off," he breathes with a smile. "Maybe I can switch you back on, too, and you can be my buddy, huh? Hopefully this building won't break you, though. We'll see."

It's strange to listen to his own voice in the silence of the arcade room. The only other thing that Levi can hear is the static of the glitches around him.

He gets back to work, finding the setting for the byts' scheduled alarms. With a few clicks, he manages to switch them all off before concentrating on their flight paths.

"All right, you first," Levi says to Beetle Bob, finding him in the database and switching him on. He fiddles around with the byt's settings, hoping that his plan to make him a bit more friendly will work. "Beetle Bob, friend mode."

Beetle Bob's eyes glow green. "Friend mode activated. Hi, Levi, how can I help you today?"

"Oh, good." Levi laughs and picks up the little byt. "How about you keep me company while we take down a villain and free the planet?"

"Sounds fun, Levi," Beetle Bob replies, fluttering his wings. "Let me know if there's anything else you need."

Levi sets Beetle Bob down on the desk and focuses on the rest of the byts. Now that he can control them, he doesn't have to do any of this by himself anymore. He doesn't have to physically go out and face Sable. He can ask them to help him with that. In fact...

"There's another way to find Juniper." Levi grins at Beetle Bob, who buzzes happily. "Let's see if I can coordinate this."

He starts working on the byts, sending a small swarm of them to each of the council buildings and the spot where the rest of the revolution members are locked up. He suspects that someone must have noticed what's going on at this point. Sable will definitely be looking for him, and so will the Monitors. They'll probably try to regain control of the byts, too.

"Hmm." Levi taps at his chin. "Beetle Bob, could you connect and build a firewall around this network to keep trespassers out?"

"Of course, Levi," Beetle Bob buzzes, plugging himself into the computer. "This will take a few moments. Please remain patient. Firewall building in progress."

"Great." At this point, Levi feels a lot more confident. At the same time, he's aware that his time is limited now. While the council won't find him digitally, there's always the possibility that they will start physically scouring the city. Eventually, they will come across this building.

Levi has to expose Sable before that happens, and he needs to find Juniper at the same time. He wishes that he had six or even eight arms so that he could type faster and on more computers.

Unfortunately, he only has the two, along with a little bug who has finally become his friend. That's better than nothing, though. Frankly, Levi is sure that's all he needs.

"Firewall 20% built, Levi," Beetle Bob announces with a squeak. "Please allow a few more minutes. No trespassers detected."

"Thank you, buddy. I knew I could count on you. Okay, they're heading for the council buildings." Levi smiles, watching the byts on the screen move through the city. "Don't worry, Juniper, we're coming for you."

Chapter 14:

Suddenly Saved

Juniper sits with her chin in her hands, bored and worried out of her mind. Levi won't be able to find her with her byt switched off. Sable has been mumbling to himself and plotting world domination, and occasionally practicing his evil laugh.

For the most part, he's been ignoring her. She's being watched by a few surveillance byts, but that's not the problem. Even if they weren't there, she doesn't think that she'd be able to get herself out of this safe.

Suddenly, the byts flash purple lights a few times.

"Alarm system disconnected," they say in unison. "Travel mode activated."

Instantly, they zoom away, right through the digital windows. Juniper stares at where they disappeared, her jaw nearly handing on the floor.

"What?" Sable notices at the last moment, blinking when he turns around. "What is going on?"

He rushes at the safe door, roaring through it at Juniper. "What have you done?"

"Uh, nothing," Juniper snaps in return. "I've literally been in here for hours, and you didn't leave me any devices to keep myself busy with. You probably messed something up on your own computer."

"Don't toy with me!" Sable shouts, storming off to stare at his own screen, only to realize that he's been locked out of every command center on the planet. "This isn't possible."

An ancient walkie-talkie hiding somewhere on his desk crackles to life. "Sable, Sable, are you there?"

"Huh?" Sable swings on his heels, trying to see where the spooky voice is coming from. "Who's that?"

"The council has decided on an emergency meeting," the voice continues, ignoring Sable's confusion. "No one has access to the usual communication channels. Please make your way to council headquarters immediately."

Sable glares at Juniper over his shoulder. "This isn't over, little girl. I know you're behind this, somehow."

Juniper shrugs, struggling to hide her smile. "Sure."

Sable leaves the penthouse in a hurried huff, and Juniper can barely contain herself. She knows exactly who is doing all of this, and she can't wait for him to succeed.

Across the city, Levi is checking every swarm of byts' surveillance cameras, scanning them all for a glimpse of Juniper. He'll work on taking down Sable as soon as he knows for sure that she's safe.

"Firewall complete," Beetle Bob announces, clearly very proud of that achievement. "Is there anything else I can do to help you, Levi?"

"How much charge do you have?" Levi asks, not wanting to push the little byt further than it can handle.

"Battery is at 55%, Levi," Beetle Bob answers. "Charge will be necessary in six hours."

"Mm, that took a lot out of you, huh?" Levi sits back in his chair for a moment. "Why don't you take a nap? You can wake up when you're back at full charge."

Beetle Bob looks at him curiously, clearly not fully understanding the command.

"I mean, go into charging mode until your battery is full." Levi laughs, remembering that Beetle Bob isn't a living being, even if he is incredibly cute. Beetle Bob makes a sound like a digital yawn nonetheless, makes a few circles, and shuts down. A red light comes on through his wings, indicating that he's charging.

"Hey, I think I saw her!" Levi redirects part of the swarm of surveillance byts in the city back to Sable's building after they pass the windows of his penthouse. "Juniper!"

Levi knows that she can't hear him, but he hopes that she'll know where these byts are coming from. He sends them right through the windows and spots her in the weird glass safe in the corner. Immediately, she gets up and puts her hands up against the door.

"Levi, are you behind this?" she asks. Levi makes the byts' eyes flash green a few times, making Juniper's face break out in a grin. "I knew you could do it! I mean, I thought you could. I really hoped it. Anyway... I don't know how I can get out of here. Sable has gone to an emergency council meeting. I think they're going to come looking for you."

Juniper is right. In the council headquarters at the center of the city, all four members have decided to pour every resource and every Monitor that they have into finding the errant colonist. Sable has, by this point, figured out that it's the child doing all of this, something he never expected. But he doesn't tell the rest of the council. They'd become suspicious about how he knows that without access to any of the networks.

"Good, so we're in agreement," Sable says at the end of the meeting. "Each of us will lead our own team into a quadrant of a city, and send four more teams out. Our number one target is whoever is breaking our system. Let's get moving."

Meanwhile, Levi is so excited about having found Juniper that he can barely contain himself. Beetle Bob is still charging, so there is no one to share his excitement with. He can't dwell on it for too long, either. Juniper needs to get out, right now.

"Okay, let's see," Levi says, typing commands for the byts in Sable's building to follow. Hopefully they'll be able to unlock the safe. At the same time, he sends out another set of byts to find the council so that he'll know how close they are to finding him.

"I wonder if I can have them talk to her," Levi ponders, searching through the settings with one hand while the other checks the status of the searching byts. "This might be a little harder than I thought."

He sighs, and sits back to think, tapping his finger on his nose. Beetle Bob is still charging, but Levi needs his help. Hopefully his battery will hold.

"Beetle Bob, can you wake up?" Levi asks, and the tiny byt immediately zooms up into action.

"Charge is at 58%," he announces. "How can I help you, Levi?"

"Please see if you can coordinate the byts in the network," Levi asks. "I need them to block the streets so that possible trespassers cannot enter this building."

Beetle Bob doesn't question that at all. Instead, he buzzes. "Network connected. Byts will be coordinated in two minutes."

"Great," Levi says, turning his attention back to Juniper's situation. It takes a bit of time, but he figures out how to give the byts commands that they will voice aloud. "Juniper, it's me. I'm going to try and unlock this thing."

"I thought you were doing that already," she says from inside, rolling her eyes. "You need to hurry. I don't know when they'll find you, but I have an idea. I just... I need to get out of here first, before I can do anything."

"Byts coordinated," Beetle Bob announces happily. "Three groups detected heading in this direction. Byts given instructions. Please stand by."

Levi's nerves are starting to run wild now. If they lock him up before he can save Juniper, then it will be over, and Sable will win. The rest of the council won't believe Levi, and they might just think that Juniper ran away. That's probably what Sable will tell them, anyway.

"Sorry," Levi makes the byts say, then has them go to work. The safe has a fairly difficult encryption system to figure out, but he's sure that he can get it done. "I'm sending one of them to check out his computer. Maybe it's in the files on there."

"Good idea," Juniper answers with a smile. "Man, I feel pretty useless. You sure there isn't anything I can do in the meantime?"

Levi feels bad about that, but she's stuck in a glass case. "No, it's okay. I've got this."

"One group diverted," Beetle Bob says from the desk. "Two groups still en route. Swarms sent to intercept."

"Thanks." Levi glances at his own byt fondly, now convinced that they can be friends. He sends some of the byts in Sable's buildings to search the villain's files for an answer to the safe.

But he's still nervous. The council members are almost here, and Juniper is still stuck. They probably only have a few minutes before someone breaks down the door and drags Levi out of here.

Levi gets up and kicks his chair out of the way, leaning in over the keyboard closely. He's too stressed to sit down.

"Groups are breaking through defenses," Beetle Bob says monotonously. He doesn't sound too worried, and Levi is jealous. Beetle Bob probably can't feel nervous at all, which makes Levi wish that he was an AI, at least in this situation. "Time to arrival, two minutes and forty-five seconds."

"Ah, that's bad." Levi bounces on his toes. One of the byts in Sable's building sends back an alert that they've accessed Sable's passwords at that moment. They know how to open the safe.

In a hurry, Levi sends them back to set Juniper free. He has to hope that this will work. Otherwise, he has no idea what to do.

Chapter 15:

A Good Compromise

"Groups diverted," Beetle Bob reports suddenly, with only thirty seconds remaining. "New estimated time of arrival, one minute and fifty seconds."

"That's great." Levi grins, breathing a sigh of relief right after. "I think we're almost there."

"I heard a click," Juniper says on the screen, and then she starts laughing when the door lights up green and swings open. "You did it, Levi!"

Levi jumps in the air and claps his hands together, struggling to believe what's just happened.

"You're free!" he yells, even though Juniper can't hear him directly.

"Group diversion failed. Estimated time of arrival, one minute." Beetle Bob interrupts the celebration with a straight face, of course.

"Oh, yeah, that." Levi scurries back to the computer and sends a new voicing command to the byts. One of them flutters up to Juniper to speak.

"Do you think you could get to that idea of yours now? I'm in a lot of trouble over here."

"Yeah, of course," Juniper answers, rushing to Sable's computer. "Can you bring the comms back online? Maybe have the byts broadcast video instead of recording it? Specifically Sable's byt. I think he forgot, but it probably recorded his whole evil rant about taking over the planet."

"Thirty seconds," Beetle Bob buzzes. This time, it seems like he actually might be nervous.

Levi starts rapidly typing commands into the computer, hoping that he doesn't make any mistakes. Sweat is pouring from his forehead, and his heart is beating wildly. This has to work. It's their last chance.

"Ten seconds."

Levi clicks a few times and sends one last voice prompt to Juniper. "You should be able to do it now."

Behind him, there's a hammering at the building's door. Sable and Hunter, another council member, burst through it, along with several Monitors.

"Put your hands up!" Hunter yells at Levi, who turns to face them, hoping that Juniper can take over from here and succeed. "You're under arrest!"

Levi does as they ask. Beetle Bob is confiscated, and Levi is put in cuffs and led outside. The whole time, Sable is smiling maliciously at him. But Sable doesn't know that Juniper is free.

As soon as the group walks out into the street, the whole city's buildings light up with images, and Juniper's voice comes on over every single loudspeaker. She fills the city with her confident tone.

"To all council members," she starts her announcement. "There is a snake among you. Sable has been trying to take over Acury and remove all of you from power. He is the one behind the Anti-Rule Revolution. We have been trying to save us all."

"What?" Hunter seems confused, and he glances at Sable, who pretends to be just as shocked.

"I have no idea what she's talking about," he insists. "I don't know how many children are running wild, but we should get them under control."

"If you don't believe me," Juniper continues, dialing up the volume on the surveillance byt's recorded video, "please join me in watching these clips of Sable admitting everything, as if he doesn't know he's being caught on camera. He thinks he can make fools of us all."

All across the city, over every screen and every window, recordings start to play of Sable giving orders to the revolution using his Sectal. He never uses Juniper's name in any of them, which Levi thinks is pretty lucky. Then, there's the video of Sable admitting everything to Juniper while she's caught in the glass safe.

His whole plan, all in his own voice, and the whole city can hear it. Levi can't stop himself from grinning.

Juniper starts talking again at the end of the video. "You've been arresting the wrong people. We've been working to uncover this devious plot. I hope that the entire council can see who the real bad guy is now. Control of the systems will be handed back once Sable is in custody and you've met us in the council headquarters."

All of the Monitors who are holding Levi are now staring at Sable, as is Hunter. Sable laughs awkwardly and shakes his head.

"Come on now. I can explain," he says, holding up his hands. "Honestly, you don't think these kids could've doctored that footage to cover their tracks?"

Hunter raises one eyebrow and nods to the Monitors. "You can explain from behind bars. Arrest him, please."

The Monitors quickly let go of Levi and reach for Sable, commanding him to put his hands behind his back.

"No, you can't do this," Sable insists angrily, as if that will get him out of this. "Let go of me! Don't you know who I am? You're going to take some rebellious child's word over mine?"

"Take him away. Make sure he doesn't escape," Hunter says to the monitors, completely ignoring Sable's protests. "And you, young boy. I assume whomever was doing the announcement wanted you to be present at this council headquarters meeting."

"Yeah, I think so," Levi answers awkwardly. "But... uh, am I going in cuffs, or..."

Hunter smiles at him and reaches over to unlock his handcuffs and return Beetle Bob to him.

"Don't try anything funny, you got that?"

"Wouldn't dream of it, Sir," Levi says with a shrug. He puts Beetle Bob in his pocket and pats the byt on the head. This isn't entirely over, but Levi's body is filled with relief already. He's so tired, all he wants to do is to sleep.

But this meeting can't wait. It's important. They have to get the other revolution members free, and they have to negotiate for Acury. Things can't go back to the way they were. That's not what they've been fighting for.

Levi watches as Sable is bundled into one of the Monitors' hover vehicles, still shouting about his innocence and blaming the kids. No one is listening to him, though. He's finally been exposed for the evil villain that he truly is. This time, there's nothing he can say that will change anyone's mind.

Hunter summons a platform, and Levi joins him on it. It's a quiet ride to the council headquarters, where a Monitor escorts the two of them up to a massive meeting hall on the top floor.

Inside, the room is surrounded by digital windows. There's a huge table in the middle with a bunch of chairs around it, which seems a little unnecessary when there are only four people on the council. Levi doesn't mention it, however, since that doesn't seem very important right now.

Juniper is already standing by one of the windows, and she turns when she hears the door open. The other two council members are seated at their places one either side of the table.

"Levi!" Juniper says, rushing to hug him. "You did it!"

"No," Levi argues when he steps back, making Juniper peer at him suspiciously. Then, he laughs. "We did it, silly. Together."

Juniper shakes her head and leads him to the head of the table, where two seats have been prepared for them.

"Point is," she says as she sits down next to him, "it was done, and now we're here, and it's time to make our voices heard."

"All right, we'll listen," Hunter says as he takes his own seat at the other end. He looks amused. "But note that we will not let everyone run rampant on this planet like they see fit. Rules are important."

Levi sighs. "Some rules, yeah, but don't you think that things have gotten just a little bit out of hand?"

"A little," Hunter admits with a smirk. "Sorry about that. I'm sure the other council members agree that we can now see the error of our ways."

The other two nod sheepishly, obviously embarrassed about this whole thing, but not entirely willing to remember it.

"So, what are you planning to do about that?" Juniper asks stubbornly, and Hunter grins as he leans forward over the table.

"We're going to negotiate, of course," he says.

"I want my byt to be my friend," Levi pipes up, making everyone laugh, and he continues when they've stopped, a little red in the cheeks. "The rest, I guess we can talk about."

"Sounds good." Hunter sits back up in the chair. "Brace yourself—this might be a long night."

Levi sighs. He would really like to have a nap.

Epilogue

It's been almost two weeks since Sable's arrest. The rest of the Anti-Rule Revolution members have been released from their incarceration. It looks like Sable himself might be sent back to Emberia to face trial.

Ever since the meeting between Juniper, Levi, and the council, the rules on Acury have relaxed a little. The only places now being watched are public, and the council have put up cameras for that. There are still schedules, but with a lot more free time.

Levi is all right with the new rules, especially since the council have allowed the byts to become colonists' friends. Turns out, the byts are useful for a lot more than just being tools of surveillance. Juniper isn't happy that they don't have total freedom, but she's not planning on starting another revolution just yet.

"Ah, fresh air," Levi says as he steps onto his brand-new balcony that evening. To thank him and Juniper for saving the planet, the council gave them each their own penthouse. It's a little big, but Levi doesn't mind. It gives him space to invent in his free time.

He's built Beetle Bob a new friend, Lucky Lucy. She's a digital ladybug who's not very good at flying, but she's nice enough. Levi hasn't quite got the hang of building wings yet.

The two of them come scurrying though the balcony doors to relax outside with Levi. Now that he doesn't have to spend an hour every night reading the RRGG, he likes to come out here to stare out at the city's neon lights.

"This is it, guys," he says to his byts. "This is the Acury that I've dreamed about since I was a little kid."

"Input not understood," Lucky Lucy says awkwardly. "Please try again with different input."

Levi sighs. He hasn't gotten round to properly setting up her AI yet. There's a lot of things she can't understand, and only a few things she can.

"Lucy, can you please bring me a glass of water?" Levi asks politely, and the ladybug scurries off. He knows that she won't. That command is linked to something else in Lucky Lucy's electronic mind.

"Are you having a good day, Levi?" Beetle Bob hops up onto the railing to face him. "Is there anything I can do to improve your experience?"

Levi peers at the byt and shakes his head. He doesn't think that Beetle Bob quite understands what it means to be a friend yet.

"Don't worry, I'm doing just fine," Levi replies as he stretches himself in the comfortable bean bag chair he's sitting on. "I'm having a great time."

Lucky Lucy scurries back out onto the balcony, dragging a blanket behind her.

"Ah, thanks, Lucy," Levi laughs as he takes it from her. "I did mean a blanket when I said water. You're clever."

Lucy buzzes on the floor and crawls onto the wall before settling next to the bean bag.

"Incoming communication for you, Levi," Beetle Bob says, tilting his head. "It is Juniper. Would you like to accept?"

"Sure." Levi shrugs. It's not that weird for Juniper to call him at night. She often has a lot of questions about Lucky Lucy or his other new inventions.

Beetle Bob projects Juniper's image onto the balcony wall, and Levi can immediately see that something's wrong. He sits up straight and frowns.

"Are you okay?" Levi asks, almost immediately nervous about what her answer's going to be. Surely they haven't decided to let Sable go or to bring new rules onto the planet. But what else could it be? Things have been going really well for weeks.

"Uh, I'm not sure," Juniper answers, her frown reflecting his. "Listen, do you think you could come over here?"

"Yeah, I'm on my way," Levi says, already hopping to his feet. "Lucy, could you go to bed?"

"Sleep mode activated." Lucky Lucy yawns, a line of z's appearing on the little screen where her eyes usually are.

"Beetle Bob, can you close everything and meet me at Juniper's?" Levi continues, summoning a platform to the balcony's edge. "Make sure the shower is off this time, too, please."

"Will do, Levi!" Beetle Bob replies as he salutes Levi with one of his six legs. Levi gets on the platform, already worried, before directing it to

Juniper's building. There are a million possibilities going through his head, but none of them seem particularly likely.

When he gets there, Juniper is already outside on her own balcony, looking frustrated and confused at the same time.

"What's up?" Levi asks as he stops near the railing and hops over. "You lose something? Forget a password? No. You probably wouldn't have asked me to come if it was something stupid. Did Sable escape or something?"

"There's something wrong with Fly Billy," Juniper replies, a tear forming in the corner of her eye. "I thought you'd be able to check him out, maybe run a diagnostic? I don't want to wait until morning to take him to maintenance. I wouldn't be able to sleep."

"Hmm, okay," Levi breathes. He was worried it would be much worse than that. Juniper heads inside and Levi follows.

Fly Billy is sitting on the floor of Juniper's bedroom, doing nothing weird at all.

"Uh," Levi starts, but Juniper interrupts him.

"Wait for it," she says. "He only does it every ten minutes or so. It's been like... eight."

Juniper stares at her byt, and so does Levi, although he's wondering if Juniper has lost her marbles.

Then, Fly Billy buzzes to life, purple lights flashing. "Incoming communication."

He vibrates some more, before Juniper speaks. "From who?"

"Incoming communication," Fly Billy repeats.

"Okay, fine, I accept it," Juniper says, sounding like she's done this a hundred times before.

Fly Billy buzzes, and then a string of random noises comes from his speakers. They sound like tapping. Sometimes fast, sometimes slow.

"I think... I recognize that," Levi whispers. "It's a really old form of communication. My mom explained it to me... It's... I think it's called Morse code, or something like that."

"If that's what it is," Juniper says, turning to him with wide eyes, "where is it coming from?"

Made in the USA
Monee, IL
30 December 2023

49611679R00063